I0531555

Kerwin is training to be a council assassin against his mother's wishes, but then he does a lot of things against his mother's wishes. The only thing she wants for him is to marry a nice demon woman and have lots of demon babies, so when he finds himself on a surprise blind date she organized, he grabs the first cute guy he finds and tells his date he has a boyfriend.

Fergus was at the coffee shop to meet his best friend, not to play fake boyfriend — to his mate? When Kerwin leaves, Fergus panics because he hasn't had the time to tell him they're fated to be together, but luckily for him, his best friend knows exactly who Kerwin is. Their problems aren't over, though.

Fergus and Kerwin are just starting to work things out when Fergus's sister gives birth to a half-demon baby she doesn't want. Fergus can't abandon his nephew, but he also can't be sure that Kerwin is ready to be not only a mate but also a father. Will he have to choose between being the two?

The unauthorized reproduction or distribution of this copy-righted work is illegal. Criminal copyright infringement, including infringement without monetary gain, is investigated by the FBI and is punishable by up to 5 years in federal prison and a fine of $250,000.

This book is a work of fiction. Names, characters, places, and incidents either are products of the author's imagination or are used fictitiously. Any resemblance to actual events or locales or persons, living or dead, is entirely coincidental.

Kerwin
Copyright © 2023 Catherine Lievens
ISBN: 978-1-4874-3892-0
Cover art by Angela Waters

All rights reserved. Except for use in any review, the reproduction or utilization of this work in whole or in part in any form by any electronic, mechanical or other means, now known or hereafter invented, is forbidden without the written permission of the publisher.

Published by eXtasy Books Inc

Look for us online at:
www.eXtasybooks.com

KERWIN
COUNCIL ASSASSINS 16

BY

CATHERINE LIEVENS

CHAPTER ONE

When Greg reached for Kerwin, Kerwin's first instinct was to grab him with his tail. It was like a third arm to him, and he was used to relying on it as much as he relied on his other appendages. The problem was that he was supposed to be learning not to rely on it that way. If he wanted to become an assassin, he needed to be able to attack and defend himself without using his tail.

Even though he hated it.

He tightened his tail around his waist and focused on defending himself with his arms instead of throwing it out at Greg. He raised one arm, blocking Greg's punch, and since he knew the other man, he could predict what Greg would do next.

Kerwin grinned. Sure enough, Greg crouched just a bit and threw out a leg, trying to kick Kerwin off balance. Kerwin unwrapped his tail from his waist and used it for balance, pressing the tip against the ground. He kept himself on his feet, then used his tail to propel himself forward.

"That's a good use of your tail," Jamison said from the sideline.

Kerwin beamed. He wanted the trainers to see he was trying, and he was glad they did. It was getting easier, and he was damn proud.

What *wasn't* getting easier was not being distracted. Kerwin didn't feel in danger when he was training with his friends, but he would be when he was in a real fight, something he hadn't yet experienced. He'd have to keep his focus then, something he wasn't doing well just now.

And Greg took advantage of it.

Greg twisted and threw out his other leg. It knocked against Kerwin's calves, and even with his tail out, the force was enough to send Kerwin backward. He circled his arms, trying to keep himself on his feet, but Greg stood in front of him with a grin. He quickly pushed Kerwin, who fell back, his ass hitting the ground.

Jamison clapped his hands. "Good job," he said.

Greg offered Kerwin his hand, and even though Kerwin was tempted to pout, he took it and allowed Greg to pull him to his feet.

"I ended up on my ass," he grumbled.

Jamison chuckled. "You did, but you made a conscious effort not to rely on your tail. Instead, you used it the way we're training you to use it. That's a win, in my book. You still have to think about not using it when you fight, but it'll become instinct, and that's what we're aiming at."

Kerwin found himself smiling. If Jamison, who was one of the trainers, told him he'd done a good job, he could believe him. None of the trainers would have said that if it hadn't been true. They were training Kerwin and the others to become council assassins, and it would be too dangerous to lie to them when it came to this.

At least someone was happy with Kerwin and how he was doing. He couldn't say the same for his mother, but then she seldom had anything to be happy about when it came to him lately. She had expectations, and unfortunately, they didn't match Kerwin's. She had a hard time understanding and wrapping her mind around that.

Kerwin followed Greg to the side of the training area. Two other trainees took their spot, and Kerwin flopped down on the grass next to Wallace. Wallace's cheeks were flushed and he was still sweating, but from what little Kerwin had seen, he'd done a good job, too.

"Payne kicked my ass," Wallace whined.

"And was Hawthorne there to see it?"

Kerwin hadn't thought it possible, but Wallace's cheeks flushed an even darker red.

"He's not here today," Wallace mumbled.

"Then it's fine, right?"

Wallace rolled his eyes. "Fine? The others saw me."

"Yeah, but you have a crush on one of our trainers. You know, both of you are adults. No one would care if something happened between the two of you."

"He'd have to allow me to get close," Wallace muttered. "But every time he sees me, he runs the other way."

Kerwin had noticed Hawthorne's behavior, but it was none of his business. He wanted his friend to be happy, and whether or not that was with Hawthorne didn't matter. He wished Hawthorne wasn't making such a visible effort to keep Wallace at arm's length, though.

Kerwin dried his face with his towel and dug into his bag for his phone. When he found it, he took it out and checked his notifications, groaning when he saw a text from his mother. Wallace leaned against him, peeking at the screen.

"I thought she wasn't talking to you," he said.

"Looks like she changed her mind." Kerwin unlocked the phone. He might as well see what his mother wanted. Trying to ignore it wouldn't help. If anything, it would make things more challenging, because she'd know he was ignoring her, and she'd be pissed.

And no one wanted to deal with her when she was pissed.

Kerwin opened the message with apprehension. He read it, frowned, then reread it. "Huh. It looks like she decided it was time for us to make peace."

"Yeah?" Wallace asked.

Both of them had complicated relationships with their

parents. In Kerwin's case, it was with his mother, while Wallace and his father didn't see eye to eye. Kerwin knew that if Wallace had his way, he wouldn't be here, training to become a council assassin. The only reason he trained was that his father was in the military and had pulled a lot of strings. He wanted Wallace to follow in his footsteps in uniform like Wallace's brothers had, even though there was nothing Wallace wanted less. Wallace's father didn't care what Wallace wanted, unfortunately. Many people would have told Wallace to tell his father to fuck off, but Kerwin could understand how hard it was to do something like that with a parent. Even though his mother was infuriating and treated him like a child who didn't know what he wanted, she was still his mother.

And apparently, she wanted to have coffee with him.

"She says she misses me and that she'd like to get coffee after training. She'll wait for me in a coffee shop in town."

"Isn't that weird?"

It kind of was, but Kerwin hoped this was a way his mother had come up with to reach out to him. She wasn't one for coffee shops, but the fact that she was willing to go to one to be with Kerwin made him smile. "I didn't expect it."

Wallace's smile was sad. "I'm glad for you."

Kerwin didn't tell Wallace his father would come around, too. He'd met the man a few times and doubted anything would make him change his mind. Wallace's unhappiness certainly hadn't.

And speaking of the devil, Kerwin winced when he noticed Wallace's father striding toward them. He wished he could shield Wallace, who hadn't seen his father yet, but there was nothing Kerwin could do. Wallace's father wasn't a man who took being ignored nicely. Kerwin doubted he took anything nicely.

"Wallace!" the man yelled.

Wallace's eyes widened, and he scrambled to his feet. He

turned to face his father as the man reached them.

Just like Wallace, Wallace's father's cheeks were flushed. It wasn't for the same reason, though. Wallace had been training, while his father was clearly pissed.

"What was that?" Wallace's father demanded to know.

"What was what?" Wallace asked.

"You called that a fight? That man kicked your ass."

Wallace looked down at his feet. "I did my best," he mumbled.

"Your best isn't enough! Why are you so intent on wasting the opportunity I gave you? Do you understand how many people wish they could be here in your place? You got one of these spots, thanks to me, but you're going to lose it if you don't take this seriously. I don't think I've ever been as disappointed in you as I am now."

Wallace glanced up. "I thought you'd been disappointed in me since I was born," he snarked.

His father's eyes narrowed, and he took a step forward. "What did you just say?" he asked, raising a hand and pushing Wallace's shoulder.

That was it. Kerwin had hesitated to intervene, because Wallace knew better than anyone how to deal with his father, but he wouldn't allow the asshole to hurt Wallace.

Hawthorne stepped in before Kerwin could do or say anything. Kerwin wasn't even sure where the man had come from. Like Wallace had said, he hadn't been here before, yet now, he suddenly was — a mountain of a man, staring down Wallace's father. Kerwin could suddenly understand why Wallace had such a crush on him.

"What do you think you're doing?" Hawthorne asked with a growl.

Kerwin noticed he stayed as far away from Wallace as possible, guiding Wallace's father to face him rather than fully going to them.

"You're one of the trainers?" Wallace's father asked.

"I am, and if you have any problem with your son's training, you come to me."

Kerwin eyed the two men, then Wallace, who looked like he wanted the earth to swallow him. Kerwin couldn't say he blamed him, and as he wrapped an arm around his friend's shoulders, he wondered what would happen next.

Wallace hated this. He didn't want to hurt people. He didn't want to be an assassin. He'd told Kerwin all of this more than once, and Kerwin's heart broke every time.

Because Wallace didn't have a choice.

"You need to eat more," Fergus's grandmother said. "You lost weight since the last time I saw you."

He patted her arm. "I haven't." Even though he'd been trying like hell to do exactly that. He liked eating a little too much, though, and he'd surrendered to the fact that he'd always have a bit of a stomach a while back. He didn't mind the way he looked, anyway.

"Are you blind?" Fergus's sister asked. "How can you say he's lost weight? It's clear he's *gained* weight."

Fergus bit his tongue. He wanted to snap back at Emily, but their mother was in the room with them, and she wouldn't let him. If he tried, she'd spend the next half hour yelling at him, and he had an appointment for coffee with his best friend. He didn't have the time or energy to deal with his mother's tantrums today. He kind of wished he didn't have to deal with his sister, either, but she wasn't going anywhere. She sat at the kitchen table, eating cake and rubbing her stomach. She was huge, but then she'd be giving birth soon.

Fergus wasn't sure if he dreaded that moment or if he couldn't wait for it to happen. He had no way to find out how becoming a mother would change Emily, but if she followed their mother's example, it would be for the worse.

Their grandmother frowned. "That's not nice," she scolded Emily.

"It wasn't meant to be. Someone has to be honest with him before he becomes as big as a house."

Fergus swallowed. Even though his sister and his mother had been talking about him this way since he was a child, it still hurt. He'd accepted himself and knew nothing was wrong with him. He wasn't the most beautiful man in the world and wasn't exactly fit, but he wasn't a monster, either. His sister was aware of that, but she liked getting under his skin, and she was extremely good at it, especially now that she had nothing else to focus on. She was reaching the end of her pregnancy, which meant she wasn't working.

Not that she'd been working before. But she'd spent most of her time with her friends, partying and doing who knew what. Fergus hadn't seen her much, and he'd been grateful.

He swallowed the bitterness that threatened to come out. "It's fine. But I have to go."

"Where?" his mother intervened. She watched him over the rim of her mug. She only drank her coffee black — like her heart.

She wasn't asking because she was curious. She wanted to know what Fergus was up to so she could criticize him.

"I'm meeting Jamison." It was better not to tell them it would be in a coffee shop. Emily would jump on the occasion to make fun of him again if he did.

"You spend a lot of time with him," Fergus's mother said.

"He's my best friend."

"That's what you always say, but I don't understand why anyone would want to spend that much time with you."

She didn't say that even though she was his mother, *she* didn't want to spend any length of time with him, but he heard the words anyway, and they hurt.

7

Fergus plastered a smile on his lips and got to his feet. "I don't really understand it, but I'm not going to argue."

"Are you in love with him? Because let me tell you, that's not going to do you any good. There's no way a man like him will ever look at someone like you."

Fergus was aware of that. Luckily, he wasn't in love with Jamison. "He's just a friend," he said for what had to be the hundredth time. His mother never believed him, and he didn't understand why.

She nodded, satisfied. "Of course he is. He couldn't be anything else."

"Since you're here, I have a favor to ask," Emily interrupted.

Fergus didn't groan, but it was a close thing. He knew what his sister wanted. "Yes?" he asked, even though he wanted to say no and run.

"I need money for the baby," Emily said. She acted as if she hadn't insulted Fergus seconds ago, but he supposed that to her, it didn't matter. She didn't see anything wrong with what she said to him.

"I don't have anything available right now. I gave you everything I could spare the other day."

"Don't talk to your sister like that," Fergus's mother snapped. "She's about to have a baby. She needs money and for people to take care of her."

Fergus wanted to ask her why *she* didn't take care of Emily, but he didn't dare. "I realize that, and I wish there was more I could do, but until I get paid, I don't have anything else." He hesitated. "Maybe you could reach out to the father, Emily."

He'd known that was a mistake even before the words left his lips, but Emily hadn't created this baby herself. She'd refused to tell anyone who the father was, and Fergus wondered if it was because she didn't know. He wouldn't be surprised, and he didn't care, but he was tired of supporting

Emily, dammit.

Emily's eyes narrowed, which told Fergus she was angry. He didn't have a lot of time to ready himself for what was coming. Seconds later, Emily pressed her hands against her face and sobbed.

It was loud and dramatic, and extremely fake.

"Look at what you've done," Fergus's mother snapped as she rushed toward Emily. She wrapped an arm around her daughter's shoulders, trying to soothe her. "I already told you not to bring the father up," she snarled at Fergus

"I know, but he should know what's happening. This is his baby, too. He should contribute."

"Who the father is doesn't matter. This is Emily's baby, which means he'll be perfect and beautiful." She glared at Fergus. "Unlike you."

That last barb was expected, and it didn't even hurt. Fergus got to his feet, ready to be out of there. "All right. I'll get you money as soon as I can."

"See that you do."

Fergus kissed his grandmother's cheek. "I'll see you soon, all right?"

She was still frowning. He knew she wished she could say something more to Emily and Fergus's mother, but the three of them lived together. They'd made her life a living hell the few times she'd tried to say anything, and Fergus had convinced her to stop. He'd take her in if he could, but his apartment was too small. She kept insisting she didn't need a babysitter, but she was older, which was why she lived with Fergus's mother, who was supposed to take care of her. He supposed she did.

In her own way.

Fergus almost ran out of the room. Being here made it hard to breathe, and he'd never come back if it weren't for his grandmother. Since she lived here, Fergus tortured himself by

9

coming around at least a couple times a week. He was always happy to see her but even happier to leave.

He climbed into his car, carefully backed out of the driveway, and made his way toward the coffee shop. He wondered what he'd order as he drove. Maybe some tea? If he got just plain tea, though, Jamison would notice, and he'd know Fergus had just seen his mother and sister. He always got pissed when that happened, so it would be better if Fergus bought what he actually wanted, which was coffee with enough caramel to drown himself. It wasn't like he drank the stuff every day, anyway. He was careful about how he ate, but he could get a good coffee.

Hopefully, the sugar would be enough to get him out of the funk he always fell into when he saw his family.

Kerwin peeked into the changing room. He wasn't surprised to see that Wallace was still there, sitting on one of the benches, staring ahead. Kerwin was pretty sure Wallace couldn't see what was in front of him. He was lost in his thoughts, which considering what had happened, wasn't a surprise.

Kerwin rapped his knuckles on the frame of the door. Wallace jerked at the sound, started getting to his feet, then relaxed when he saw it was Kerwin.

"Everything okay?" Kerwin asked, even though it was clear everything wasn't.

Wallace shrugged. "I'll be fine. It's not the first time he's talked to me like that."

Kerwin hesitated. Wallace was a private person, but what had happened today had made Kerwin both scared and angry. "Does he always become physical?"

The way Wallace avoided looking at Kerwin told Kerwin he did.

"Sometimes, when he's really pissed," Wallace confirmed. "He doesn't care that I'm training to kill people. Apparently, he doesn't think I'd be able to kill him."

Kerwin went to sit next to Wallace. "I know you don't like talking about this, but I'm here if you need me. What your father is doing isn't right. He shouldn't force you to do this or anything else. No one should, especially considering what this training will lead to. You don't have it in you to kill people."

Wallace snorted. "Because you do? None of us know what it'll be like once we become assassins. We think we do and want to do the right thing, but I'm pretty sure several of us will take a step back once we're faced with reality."

Like Wallace would if he could. There was nothing Kerwin could say to convince Wallace to leave the program. Wallace's father wouldn't let him, and even though Wallace was an adult, his father could make his life hell.

"You don't have to stay with me," Wallace said, knocking his shoulder against Kerwin's. "Call me once your date with your mother is over, all right?"

"I'll let you know what she wanted." Kerwin wanted to be hopeful, but he was afraid to.

After stamping a kiss on Wallace's temple, Kerwin got to his feet and left the changing rooms. He'd already showered and dressed, so he headed for his car.

It was more than twenty years old, but he loved the damn thing. His mother didn't and kept telling him he needed to get a new car and hinting at the fact that she wouldn't trust this one to carry her grandchildren, but Kerwin had no intention of becoming a father any time soon. He didn't even have a significant other, although his mother was working on fixing that, which was one of the reasons they'd fought. She kept mentioning daughters of people she knew, all of them demons, of course. She wanted Kerwin's marriage to pull the entire family up the demon hierarchy, while Kerwin couldn't care less about that. He only cared about marrying someone he loved, but that wasn't the way his mother saw it.

He pushed those thoughts away. He didn't want to start fighting with his mother as soon as he saw her. She was trying to build a bridge between them, and he wouldn't be the one to tear it down.

He and the other trainees lived onsite, and while there wasn't much to the base, there was a small town nearby. It was good enough for them to take a day off when they could, and Kerwin had visited the coffee shop more than once. He was pretty sure he'd mentioned it to his mother, which was no doubt why she'd chosen it place.

Kerwin was already dreaming of a nice chai tea as he parked his car and headed inside the coffee shop. The smell of coffee was strong when he walked in, and he took a deep breath, a smile forming on his face. Even if his mother was here to fight again, it would be worth it.

He looked around, but she wasn't there yet, so he went to the counter to get his drink. Before he could get there, a woman got to her feet and waved at him.

He cocked his head. She was a demon, her tail and the blue swirls on her skin making it obvious, but he was pretty sure he didn't know her. It was kind of surprising to see a demon here. Kerwin was one of the few, and he doubted any demon lived in town.

He narrowed his eyes. The woman was still staring at him, clearly expecting him to do something. He was tempted to ignore her, but he suspected that wouldn't stop her. He might as well get this out of the way. If he was lucky, she'd confused him with whoever she was waiting for.

"Hi," she said when he reached her table. She sat back down and wrapped her fingers around her cup of coffee.

She wore a white dress with a blue cardigan that

complimented the swirls on her skin and her blue hair. She was pretty, but not Kerwin's type. She seemed too perfect, almost doll-like.

"Do I know you?" he asked.

She frowned, then smiled sweetly. "Well, I expected your mother to at least show you the picture I sent her, but I suppose that's fine. I'm Maribel."

Kerwin still had no idea what she was talking about, but his stomach churned at the mention of his mother. "I'm supposed to meet my mother."

Maribel looked confused. "Your mother? No. She told me you'd agreed to go on a date with me today. That's why you're here, yes? I'm not usually one for blind dates, but your mother said so many wonderful things about you, and you're as cute as she said."

Maribel glanced down as if embarrassed while Kerwin tried to make sense of what she'd said.

She believed he was here to go on a date with her, not because he was meeting his mother for coffee. His mother, who would rather be dead than get caught in a coffee shop. His mother, who'd been trying to set him up with various demon women because she wanted him to get married, stop training as a council assassin, and settle down. She'd demanded grandkids the last few times they'd talked, and even though he'd told her he wasn't planning on having any right now, she clearly hadn't given up.

Kerwin wasn't here to see his mother. That was a lie. She'd told him to meet her because she'd known he wouldn't come otherwise, but this had always been a blind date with Maribel.

Dammit.

Kerwin would make sure his mother knew how he felt about all of this as soon as he saw her, but first, he needed to let Maribel down nicely. She had no idea what was going on, and he didn't want to hurt her.

"I'm sorry," he started. He eyed the door, wondering what

Maribel would say if he ran. "My mother told me to come here to have coffee with her. She never mentioned you."

Maribel's expression turned confused. "What? So you *didn't* want to take me out on a date?"

"I'm sorry, but I didn't even know you existed until now. My mother just said she wanted to see me and gave me the time and place, and I came." He looked up at the sound of the door opening. A pretty man came in, and he was much more Kerwin's type.

His brown hair shone under the coffee shop lights, and his brown eyes were wide as he looked around. His nose was a touch long, but it gave character to his face.

Kerwin stepped toward the man, who looked up in question. Kerwin silently prayed the guy would forgive him and wouldn't try to punch him as he grabbed his hand and pulled him toward Maribel, who was staring at them with wide eyes.

"I'm really sorry," Kerwin told her. "I thought I was meeting my mother, and I was planning on introducing her to my boyfriend." Kerwin raised the man's hand and placed a kiss against it.

He'd be lucky if the guy didn't punch him.

Fergus had no idea what was happening. He'd tried pulling his hand away after the demon had kissed it, but the guy turned pleading eyes to him.

Fergus almost lost himself in those eyes. He leaned closer, all thoughts of getting away vanishing. The demon grinned, released Fergus's hand, and wrapped an arm around his waist before turning his attention back to the demon lady sitting at the table.

"I should have told my mother, but it was supposed to be a surprise. She didn't know about him," the demon said.

The woman was still staring, and Fergus stared back. His

mind was trying to make sense of what was happening, but it was stuck on one detail.

With the demon's arm around him, there was no way for Fergus not to smell him. Demons didn't have mates. That didn't mean demons weren't mates to shifters, which was what was happening here.

The demon was Fergus's mate.

"You mean you have a boyfriend?" the woman asked.

Fergus had to go along with this now. He still had no idea what was happening, but it was fairly easy to understand. For some reason, Fergus's mate needed this woman to believe he had a boyfriend. Fergus wasn't sure why he'd chosen him of all the people in the room, but he wasn't about to complain.

Instead, he leaned forward, offering the woman his hand. "I'm Fergus."

The woman stared at him for a moment before shaking his hand. "Maribel. I'm sorry, but I think there's been a misunderstanding. I was supposed to be on a date with Kerwin, but I had no idea he had a boyfriend."

Now that Fergus knew his mate's name, he relaxed a little bit more. "Not a problem. From what I understand, Kerwin's mother organized this."

Maribel nodded. "She did."

"Well, she didn't know about me. That was the point of meeting her today. I'm sure she'll be sorry she dragged you into this."

Maribel smiled. "Well, I'm sorry about all of this." She got to her feet and grabbed her bag from the chair next to hers. "It would be better if I left."

Fergus wasn't about to ask her to stay. He wanted answers and wouldn't get them until Maribel was gone.

"I'm really sorry," Kerwin said again, stepping away from Fergus. "It was a pleasure to meet you, though."

Maribel looked from him to Fergus. "I don't know if it was,

but good luck."

From how she said it, it was clear she knew they would need it.

Why? Would Kerwin's mother be against him having a shifter mate? From the person she'd chosen to go on a date with her son, it was clear she wanted him to stick to demons, possibly females. That was exactly the opposite of Fergus, which might prove to be a problem.

Both he and Kerwin watched Maribel leave. As soon as the door closed behind her, Fergus took a step away and turned to Kerwin.

"I'm really sorry about all of this," Kerwin said before Fergus could speak. "I'll get you coffee to thank you."

Fergus almost said no, but Jamison wasn't here yet, and he still craved that caramel. "That would be great."

Kerwin's smile was blinding. "Great. Get anything you want. I can't thank you enough for what you did." He rubbed the back of his neck. His tail was wrapped around his waist, but Fergus couldn't look away.

Of all the mates he'd ever imagined he could have, none of them had been a demon. He didn't have anything against demons, but they were all so interesting and good-looking that he couldn't see himself with one. Fate seemed to have a sense of humor, although Fergus wasn't crazy about the fact that *he* seemed to be the butt of the joke.

"You didn't want to go on a date with Maribel?" he asked as they moved toward the counter.

"I didn't even know I was meeting her. I thought I was meeting my mother, but she failed to mention Maribel. Knowing her, she thought that once I was here, I wouldn't be able to get out of the date because I wouldn't want to hurt Maribel's feelings."

"So you grabbed the first guy who came through the door and decided to make him your boyfriend."

Kerwin laughed. "I guess. I'm Kerwin, by the way."

He offered his hand, and Fergus took it. "Fergus."

Fergus's hand shook, and Kerwin frowned, but Fergus had no idea what to do or say. Should he tell Kerwin they were mates? He probably wouldn't be able to find him again if he didn't, but he didn't want Kerwin to get angry. If he'd rejected a woman like Maribel, what were the odds that he'd happily accept a man like Fergus?

Before Fergus could decide what to do, Kerwin's phone rang. He grimaced and slid it out of his jeans pocket, answering quickly.

"What did you do?" he asked the person on the other side.

Fergus inched closer so he could listen to the other side of the conversation. It was incredibly rude, but he was curious and wanted to know as much as he could about his mate before telling him what they were to each other.

"*Me*? What did *you* do? I just got a call from Maribel, and she told me you came in with a *boyfriend*?" a woman screeched.

"What was I supposed to do?" Kerwin asked. "I thought I was meeting you for coffee, not that I was going on a date with someone I can never fall in love with."

"How would you know that you can't if you didn't even give her a chance?"

"She's a woman. I'm gay. That should be enough for you to understand that Maribel isn't my type."

Kerwin paid for their drinks, grabbed his, and smiled at Fergus. He pulled the phone away from his ear for a moment, clearly not caring about what his mother was saying.

"It was a pleasure to meet you, and I'm really sorry I pulled you into this. Thank you."

He was saying goodbye. Fergus needed to stop him, but how? Could he blurt out that Kerwin was his mate while Kerwin was on the phone with his mother?

17

He stared at Kerwin's retreating back, panic seizing his chest. He needed to stop Kerwin. He'd never find him again otherwise, and Kerwin was the only chance he had to have a mate.

The door opened as Kerwin reached it. He was still on the phone, but he looked up and smiled at Jamison, who patted his shoulder. Fergus could only stare. Did Jamison know Kerwin? Maybe they worked together. Jamison had never given details about what he did because it was top secret, and Fergus had never been interested enough to ask. Maybe it was time he did so.

"Hey," Jamison said as he reached Fergus. He wrapped an arm around Fergus's shoulders and kissed the top of his head. "What were you doing, talking to Kerwin?"

Fergus turned to him, his coffee forgotten on the counter. "You know him?"

Jamison looked startled. "I do. Why?"

"How do you know him? Who is he?"

"One of the guys I train. What's going on? Did he do something to you?"

Fergus shook his head. He looked back at where Kerwin had disappeared, relieved that even though he hadn't been able to talk to him, he had a way to find him. "He didn't do anything."

"What is it, then? Because you don't look well. Did you visit your family before coming here?"

Fergus winced. He hadn't planned on telling Jamison.

"Fergus," Jamison said with a sigh. "Why do you do that to yourself? You know they never have anything nice to say."

"I know, but they're my family, and Emily is pregnant."

Jamison shook his head. "And soon she'll give birth to the spawn of Satan. You need to stay away from them."

"You know I'm not going to do that."

"I do. Why don't you tell me about Kerwin? What

happened between the two of you? And don't tell me nothing, because I'm not blind. You looked like you were panicking until you found out I knew him."

Fergus licked his lips. He didn't have secrets with Jamison except for what Jamison did for a living, and he wasn't going to start now when his best friend was the one person who could tell him how to get to Kerwin.

"He's my mate."

CHAPTER TWO

K erwin was reviewing some of the notes he'd taken during the last lesson when he heard someone call out his name. He looked up, blinking at the sun in his eyes. Whoever was calling him wasn't training with him and the others, so he looked around, curious.

Wallace bumped their shoulders together. "Are you in trouble?"

"Why would I be?"

"Don't know. Why does Jamison want to talk to you?"

Kerwin finally managed to spot Jamison, who apparently was the person calling for him. "I have no idea. I don't think I've done anything I shouldn't have." If he'd been anywhere else, he'd have thought his mother had found him, but she didn't have the facility's phone number and didn't know where it was. Kerwin planned to keep it that way. She opposed him working for the council in any way, shape, or form, and while she didn't know what he would be doing once he was done training, she knew that was where he'd end up eventually. Kerwin hadn't been allowed to tell her more, and he wouldn't have even if he could. The less she knew about what he was doing, the better it was for everyone, especially him.

But none of that explained what Jamison wanted from him.

Kerwin got to his feet as Jamison reached him. "You're looking for me?"

Jamison nodded. "I am. Can you come to my office?"

"Is there a problem?"

Thankfully, Jamison smiled. "No. You're doing well, and there are no problems. I just need to talk to you for a moment." He hesitated. "Actually, someone else needs to talk to you."

Kerwin's stomach churned. "Please tell me my mother isn't here."

Jamison looked startled and laughed. "Not as far as I'm aware. How would she know about this place?"

"I haven't told her, if that's what you're asking."

"I wasn't. I know all of you take the secrecy seriously. I do, too, as do the other trainers."

"What is it, then?" Kerwin started putting everything away in his backpack as he waited for Jamison to answer.

"Someone needs to talk to you. You'll understand more once you see him."

"You're being mysterious. I feel like I should worry."

"I'd never allow anyone or anything to hurt you or the other trainees. You're under my protection, as long as you're working here."

Jamison sounded serious, and Kerwin believed him. He hadn't really thought Jamison would allow anyone to hurt him, and he was kind of sorry he'd teased him. He was a little worried, though. He didn't like not knowing what was happening.

He waved at Wallace as he followed Jamison away from the outside training area. Wallace stared at him for a moment, but just then, Hawthorne yelled something at Payne, who was sparring with Vivian, and it distracted him. Kerwin snickered. He wondered if Wallace would ever have the guts to go up to Hawthorne and tell him how he felt. Probably not, if anything because Hawthorne was kind of intimidating. He was also observant, so Kerwin was ready to bet he knew about Wallace's crush on him.

"So my mom really isn't here?" he asked Jamison.

"I probably shouldn't stick my nose into this, but why are you so afraid that your mother could be here?"

Kerwin sighed. "We had a massive fight yesterday. She told me she wanted to meet me for coffee, and since we'd had another fight previously, I thought she wanted to make amends and tell me she was sorry. Instead, I found out she'd organized a blind date for me."

"Blind dates aren't always horrible."

"I guess this one wasn't. The lady was nice, but she was a woman, which is kind of a problem since I'm gay. I guess what hurt me the most was that my mother lied to me. She said she wanted to see me, and instead, she organized a date."

"Would things have been better if that woman had been a guy?"

"Somewhat. I probably wouldn't have asked a random guy to be my fake boyfriend if she'd done that. My mother has specific goals for me and hates that I made different choices."

Jamison grunted. "Parents are hard to deal with."

"Yeah."

Sometimes, it was easier for Kerwin to lose himself in his training. It wasn't that he didn't want to spend time with his mother or to talk to her, but every time he did, they ended up fighting because she wanted him to live the life she wanted for him, not the life he wanted for himself. She didn't understand why he wished to work for the council, why he couldn't change and like women rather than men. She wanted grandkids and didn't believe he could give them to her if he didn't marry a woman. Kerwin had told her that he had no intention of marrying anyone, and she'd started crying. She acted as if not having grandchildren was horrible and hurt her, and maybe it did, but she still couldn't force him to marry someone she chose for him.

She sure was trying, though.

When they reached Jamison's office, he opened the door

and gestured for Kerwin to walk in. Kerwin was tense, then relaxed when he saw the room was empty. "I thought you wanted me to meet someone."

"I do, but I'd like to talk to you first. Sit down."

Kerwin obeyed, even more nervous now. "Seriously, if I did something wrong, just tell me."

Instead of sitting behind his desk, Jamison sat on the edge of it on the side where Kerwin was sitting. They were close enough that Kerwin's knee brushed against Jamison's calf when he moved.

"You're not in trouble. Do you remember the guy at the coffee shop yesterday?"

"Of course." Kerwin wouldn't have been able to forget him even if he'd tried. He'd left the cafe when he took his mother's call, which was when he'd crossed paths with Jamison, but now he regretted not getting Fergus's number, and there was nothing he could do to change that. He supposed he could try going back and hoping Fergus would be there some time, but it would make him feel a bit like a creeper.

"Fergus is my best friend."

Kerwin blinked. "You know him?"

"I do. We grew up together. He was my neighbor, and we've been friends since childhood. I was at the coffee shop to meet him yesterday and was surprised to see you there."

"Damn. Did he tell you what happened?"

"He did. I'm not angry at you, and even if I was, it would be none of my business. Fergus is an adult, and he can stand up for himself."

"What is it, then? Because while I understand what you're saying, none of this is helping me relax."

"I'm just trying to find the right way to say this. Like I was explaining, Fergus is important to me. He's my best friend, so I know his family as well as him. I'm not going to sugarcoat this. They're assholes, and they've been treating Fergus badly since he was a kid."

Kerwin was sorry to hear that, but he still wasn't sure why Jamison was telling him. "All right."

Jamison shook his head. "I'm making a mess out of this. Anyway, Fergus is here and would like to talk to you. I won't let him in until you say it's all right, and I don't want you to feel obligated. He'll understand if you'd rather go back to your training."

Kerwin blinked. Fergus was *here*? He wanted to talk to him? He wouldn't say no, because he wanted to talk to Fergus, too, but it still struck him as weird. Kerwin hadn't thought he'd ever see Fergus again, and he was happy to have a chance to thank him again and ask for his number, but he wasn't sure *why* Fergus had used his relationship with Jamison to get to him.

Why had Jamison even allowed Fergus in the facility? It wouldn't make sense for Fergus to be aware of what was happening here. Jamison had to keep it a secret like the trainees and anyone else who worked here. Yet Fergus was here, and he was here for Kerwin.

Jamison sighed. "It's nothing bad," he said. "Fergus couldn't hurt a fly even if he tried. He's a good person who, unfortunately, was handed a bad family. They're pigeon shifters."

That sounded adorable, but it still didn't help Kerwin. "I can talk to him if you want me to."

"You'll talk to him if *you* want to. Like I said, I won't force you to do anything that makes you uncomfortable. I know what he wants to tell you, and it's important enough that I agreed to organize this meeting. It doesn't have anything to do with your professional life or your mother, as far as I'm aware." Jamison grinned at the last words.

Kerwin could only grin back. "I'll talk to him," he confirmed.

There wasn't a reason for Fergus to be here that Kerwin could think of, and he was curious. Hopefully, whatever Fergus had come for wouldn't spell trouble.

And if it did, Kerwin supposed he'd face it when it happened.

Fergus bounced his knee. He wanted to go in there and talk to Kerwin, but Jamison had talked him into letting him talk to Kerwin first. It was hard to stay away, though. Kerwin was Fergus's mate, and Fergus hadn't been able to stop thinking about that since he'd found out yesterday.

What would Kerwin think of it? Would he be okay being a shifter's mate? Would he wish it wasn't so?

Fergus wouldn't find out until Jamison came to fetch him, and he wasn't sure whether he was more anxious or excited about what was about to happen.

He smoothed down his shirt and resisted the urge to go to the bathroom again to look at himself in the mirror. He'd been careful when he'd gotten ready before leaving his apartment, but unfortunately, no matter what clothes he wore, there was no hiding how he looked. He was a plain-looking guy who could have been fitter, which meant he wasn't most people's type.

That might not matter. Kerwin was Fergus's mate, which meant that, in theory, Fergus was perfect for him. Fergus couldn't help but wonder if that would prove out. He was tempted to leave, but he'd promised Jamison he'd do this, and he didn't want to go before talking to Kerwin. A rejection would hurt, but what if that wasn't what Kerwin did? What if Kerwin was willing to give Fergus a chance?

Fergus couldn't give up on his mate, no matter how terrified he was of the entire situation. Kerwin would be his only mate, and he couldn't waste this opportunity. He also didn't want to take it away from Kerwin, even though, as a demon, Kerwin probably wouldn't know it had happened.

The sound of footsteps made Fergus jump up from the chair he'd been trying to stay in. He smoothed his hair down, then his shirt, and was wondering if he should smooth down his jeans when the door opened.

Jamison peeked in. He'd made Fergus wait in an office belonging to one of the other trainers so Kerwin wouldn't see him right away. Fergus had been puzzled, but he understood after Jamison had explained.

"He agreed to talk to you," Jamison said.

Fergus sucked in a breath. He could do this.

Right?

Jamison smiled as he came closer and clutched Fergus's shoulder. "Stop worrying so much. He's your mate. He's young and has some personal trouble with his mother, but it doesn't mean he's going to reject you. Give him a chance. More importantly, give yourself a chance. You're a catch, even though you don't realize it."

Fergus almost snorted, but he already knew what would happen if he did. It wasn't the first time he and Jamison had this conversation, and he wasn't willing to have it again, especially not here.

Jamison shook his head. "Every time we talk about this, I hate your mother and sister a little more. You're sure you won't let me kill them?"

"I can't allow you to get yourself in trouble, but I might take you up on your offer eventually." Because even if everything went well with Kerwin, Fergus already knew that wouldn't happen with his mother and his sister.

They'd never expected him to meet someone special who could love him, but if they had, they'd have wanted him to be with another shifter, not a demon. They were going to be horrified, and the thought was enough to make Fergus grin. He liked disappointing them. At this point, he felt he would no matter what, so he might as well lean into it.

"Stop wasting time and go get your mate," Jamison said as he gently pushed Fergus toward the door.

Wasting time wouldn't help Fergus feel better, so he sucked in a breath and stepped out into the hallway. Jamison followed him, closing the office door, but instead of going back to his office, after patting Fergus's shoulder, he headed the other way, probably to help the people Fergus had seen training out there. He'd been curious enough to ask questions, but Jamison hadn't told him anything.

Fergus walked toward Jamison's office. The door was open, and he could see Kerwin pacing up and down. He took a moment to look at his mate, and once again, he marveled at the fact that fate had chosen Kerwin for him. Kerwin was the most handsome person Fergus had ever seen. Maybe he was biased, but he didn't think so.

Kerwin was younger than Fergus, or at the very least, younger-looking. Fergus was young as a shifter, being only thirty-five, but Kerwin looked even younger. He was taller than Fergus by a couple of inches, with short hair that bordered between yellow and green. Swirls of the same color decorated his skin, and Fergus remembered yesterday that his eyes were yellow-green and black. Kerwin's tail was wrapped around his waist, and he wore the same uniform Fergus had seen on people he'd walked past earlier. Clearly, Kerwin didn't work here, but rather he was a student or something like that.

Fergus must have made a noise, because Kerwin startled and turned toward him. To Fergus's surprise, when Kerwin recognized him, he smiled, and his body instantly relaxed. His shoulders slumped, and he stopped pacing.

Fergus took a step into the office without meaning to. The draw between them was strong, and he hoped Kerwin wouldn't deny it, even though he couldn't feel it the same way Fergus did.

"Hey," Kerwin said. "I have to say I was surprised when Jamison told me you were here and that you wanted to talk to me. I didn't think I'd ever see you again, and I was kicking myself for not getting your number."

Fergus's stomach fluttered. "Really?"

"Really. I should have, and I shouldn't have allowed my mother to distract me."

Fergus closed the door. That left him and Kerwin alone, and for a moment, he panicked. Then he reminded himself that Kerwin was his mate. He might not feel the bond as strongly as Fergus, but he still felt it, and the phone number confession was proof of that.

"I was relieved when I realized Jamison knew you," he explained.

"He said you're his best friend."

"I am. We were meeting at the coffee shop. That's why I was there."

"Well, I'm happy we have a second chance to get to know each other. Jamison said you needed to tell me something, though, and it's making me nervous. Do you mind explaining what this is about?"

It was Fergus's turn to pace the room. He didn't think he could say this sitting down. He needed to get the words out, which was easier to do when he wasn't looking at Kerwin.

"Jamison told you I'm a shifter?" he asked.

"Yeah. He said you and your family are pigeon shifters, and I think that's cute, even though I don't understand why he said it."

"It's because since I'm a shifter, I have a mate."

It only took Kerwin a couple of seconds to understand what Fergus was saying. When he did, his eyes widened, and he took a step back.

Fergus steeled himself for rejection, even though it was

perfectly normal for Kerwin to be stunned by the revelation. Anyone would have been.

"I'm your mate?" Kerwin asked.

"You are. I'm sorry to tell you like this, but I wasn't sure how else to do it. It's something you need to know, even if you decide to reject me. I'm sorry to spring this on you, but you don't have to say yes to being with me. I know mates usually are, but I won't force you into anything you don't want or aren't ready for. I mean, that would make me too much like my mother, and it's not something I want to happen."

Kerwin snorted. "She's a piece of work, too?"

Fergus found himself smiling. "She is. I guess that while we were unlucky with mothers, we were lucky with our mate." It was a gamble to say that, but Fergus wanted Kerwin to know that he was happy with the mate Fate had given him.

Kerwin stared. There was no way for Fergus to know what he was thinking, but he'd said his piece. He moved toward the desk, flopped down into a chair, and waited.

Kerwin didn't know what to say. Having Fergus tell him he was his mate was the last thing he'd expected, and his brain couldn't make sense of the words. He'd heard them, but that didn't mean he understood them.

Kerwin was a demon. He didn't have a mate, something his mother was happy about because she found it ridiculous. She believed that love had little to do with marriage, which wasn't a surprise, since her marriage to Kerwin's father had been organized by their parents. Things were changing, but she was trying to push tradition on Kerwin and convince him to marry whatever woman she chose for him.

That was never going to happen, especially now that Kerwin had found out he was Fergus's mate.

So what should he do with the news?

He looked at Fergus, who'd sat down and was bouncing his knee. It was clear he was nervous, and Kerwin wondered if he'd expected a rejection. He wasn't about to reject Fergus, although he did want some time to wrap his mind around all of this. He hadn't expected to have a mate, but he wasn't going to refuse the bond just because it was unexpected. He'd seen some of his friends with their mates and how happy they were, and he wasn't about to waste that opportunity just because he didn't fully understand and was afraid.

He went to sit on the other chair, careful not to touch Fergus. He felt like if he did, everything would shatter.

"I'm sorry I shocked you," Fergus whispered. "I guess I could have kept this a secret, but I felt you deserved to know, even though you're not a shifter, or maybe especially because you're not. I realize you might not want a relationship with me, and I'll understand. You never thought you had a mate, and you don't know how to deal with it now that you do. You can just walk away." He softly snorted. "No one will be surprised if you do."

Kerwin frowned. "What do you mean?"

"Nothing."

"That doesn't sound like nothing." And Kerwin remembered what Jamison had said about Fergus's family. They were horrible, and maybe they had something to do with the way Fergus talked about himself.

"It's just that my mother and sister never believed I'd find my mate."

"Why not? I thought every shifter wanted to meet theirs."

"They don't really care. To be honest, they don't care about anyone but themselves, so I'm not surprised. They think it's outdated and stupid and don't want to feel linked to someone that way."

"What about you?"

Fergus finally looked up. His eyes looked damp, and

Kerwin had to resist the sudden urge to pull him into his arms.

"I want a mate," Fergus admitted. "Even though I didn't think I'd find him—*you*—or that you'd accept me, I always dreamed of having someone who would love me no matter what."

That was what Fergus's mother should be doing, but clearly, both he and Kerwin had problems with their parental figures. Kerwin couldn't say he was looking forward to meeting Fergus's family, because they didn't sound nice, but the same could be said about his mother.

None of them had anything to do with the situation, though. They had no say in whether or not Kerwin accepted the bond and decided to be in a relationship with Fergus. The only ones who could decide about their relationship were the two of them, and Fergus was leaving that decision in Kerwin's hands.

Kerwin might be confused, but he knew what he *didn't* want.

They could work out what he did want together.

He leaned even closer and gently brushed Fergus's hand. He wanted to take it, but Fergus looked nervous enough to explode. "I don't think I'm ready to bond right now," he admitted.

Fergus's eyes went wide. "Did I give the impression that I wanted to bond right away? Because if I did, I didn't mean to. I'm not ready to bond, either. To be honest, I'm not sure what I'm ready for."

Fergus was clearly the kind of person who blurted anything that went through their mind when they were nervous. It was endearing and adorable, and Kerwin had a hard time believing that the man sitting in front of him was supposed to be his.

How had he gotten so lucky?

This time, he did take Fergus's hand. He linked their fingers together and squeezed, which had the unintended reaction of shutting Fergus up. He squeaked and pressed his lips together, his eyes wide as he stared.

"I'm not ready to bond," Kerwin repeated. "All of this was a surprise, and I'm still unsure what to make of it. I'm not going to reject you, though, and I want to see where this goes. Would you be okay with dating for a while?"

Fergus swallowed heavily. "Anything you want."

It was nice to hear that, but Kerwin shook his head. "No. If we're going to be in a relationship, it has to be what we *both* want, not just me. I'm not going to dump you because you say something I disagree with or because you want to do something I'm not ready for. Both our feelings and wants are valid."

Kerwin knew how it felt not to be respected. He didn't want Fergus to feel like that or for their relationship to start that way. He had no idea where things would go, but it was important that he knew how Fergus felt and what he wanted.

Fergus stared for a moment before nodding. "All right. I'll tell you what I want."

Kerwin breathed easier. "I'm listening."

Fergus looked away as if embarrassed. "Like I was saying, no one expected me to meet my mate. I thought about what would happen if I did, but I never considered it a real possibility. Now that it's happened, I'll admit I'm a bit confused. I want to get to know you. I don't think we need to rush into anything, and I don't want us to. I don't want to make mistakes that would push us apart. I don't know if this is going to work, but I definitely want to try."

"That's all I want, too."

Fergus still looked surprised, which bothered Kerwin. He didn't want Fergus to think about what his family would say about this, so he leaned closer and pressed a kiss to Fergus's cheek.

Fergus squeaked again.

"Why don't you give me your phone number?" Kerwin suggested. "That way, we can text or call each other. We can decide where and when we want to go for our first date, and we can start getting to know each other."

Fergus was staring. "I can't believe this is happening," he whispered.

"Neither can I, but I know several mated couples. I didn't think I'd ever have this kind of love in my life, but you're giving me that chance, and I can never thank you enough."

"You don't have to thank me. You're my mate as much as I'm yours. You're giving me something I never thought I'd have, too."

That didn't make much sense. Fergus seemed young, although Kerwin knew that with shifters, the way they looked didn't often have much to do with their age. Still, Fergus couldn't be that old, which meant he had decades to find his mate. Why had he been so convinced he never would? It probably had something to do with the way his mother and sister treated him. They sounded dismissive, and since Jamison didn't like them, it probably meant Kerwin wouldn't, either.

Fergus needed people on his side, and Kerwin had been made for that. He wasn't going anywhere, no matter what anyone thought. Fergus was the only person who could send him away, and Kerwin doubted his mate would do that.

Fergus had come into this situation expecting to be rejected. It would have made sense, considering the state of his other relationships. He'd never known his father, but his mother had made sure he knew that he'd left before Fergus was even born. She said he hadn't wanted Fergus, but Fergus suspected it was more than that. If he'd been in his father's place, he wouldn't have wanted to be linked to his mother for life, either. He blamed his father for abandoning him, but at the same time, he could understand why he had. He didn't like it, but it didn't change anything. He wouldn't get his father back, especially since he barely knew the man's name.

His mother and his sister had always made a point of telling him how much they disliked him. They still did, but then they asked him to do things for them in their next sentence. He was too weak to say no, because he was terrified of losing the only family he had.

His grandmother.

She was the only one who'd always loved him. She'd taken care of him as he grew up, and he wanted to take care of her now that she was getting older, but she was stuck with Fergus's mother. Fergus had tried hinting at moving her into his apartment, even though it was tiny, but his mother had accused him of trying to get his grandmother's inheritance.

He'd almost laughed in her face. What inheritance was there to steal? Fergus's mother and his sister had gotten their hands on every single penny they could, and Fergus was pretty sure Grandma would never see it again.

Fergus suspected things would get even worse now that Emily was about to give birth. She and their mother would either spoil the child in a way no child should be spoiled or neglect him. And if Emily's behavior was anything to go by, she wouldn't be a great mother. Fergus wanted to help the poor child, because otherwise he'd grow up terribly, but he had no say in any of it.

He did have a say in whether or not he wanted to be with Kerwin, and he did. Kerwin was offering him the chance to date, get to know him, and eventually fall in love with him.

How could Fergus say no to that?

"You really want to date me?" He needed to be sure.

"I wouldn't have said so if I didn't. You don't seem happy,

though."

Fergus quickly looked at his mate. "I am. I just didn't expect you to want this."

"Why? Because I'm a demon and not supposed to have a mate?"

"In part. The other part is that I know I'm not much. You could have better, even if that person isn't your mate."

Kerwin was still holding Fergus's hand, and Fergus didn't want him to stop. He'd never realized that holding hands could feel so good, and he lost himself in the feeling a little until he realized Kerwin was still staring.

"What?" he asked.

"You don't have much self-esteem," Kerwin said.

He'd said it matter-of-factly, and Fergus snorted. Of course his mate had already seen that. "It's hard to develop self-esteem when people tell you every day that you're not worth anything."

"Your mother?"

"And my sister."

"What about your father?"

"I never knew him. He left before I was born, and I don't blame him. My mother is a monster."

"How about you agree not to believe anything that comes out of your mother's mouth? I don't think that anything she has to say will be beneficial to you, and besides, what she thinks doesn't matter when it comes to us."

Kerwin was right. No matter what Fergus's mother said or thought, Kerwin was the only one Fergus should listen to. He was the one involved in the relationship, after all. "All right," Fergus whispered.

That got him a smile from Kerwin. "You want to date, then?"

"More than anything." Maybe he sounded too eager, but he couldn't play games with Kerwin. He was still trying to deal with the fact that he'd found his mate. His heart was tender, ready to love, and vulnerable.

Kerwin's smile widened. "You've got yourself a boyfriend, then." He frowned. "Wait. Can I call myself your boyfriend? I mean, I'm your mate, even though we aren't bonding yet and we're dating. Shouldn't I introduce myself as your mate, then? Or would that confuse people and make them believe we're bonded?"

Fergus wanted to kiss Kerwin. Normally, he wouldn't have dared, but Kerwin had kissed his cheek earlier, and Fergus had loved it. So he quickly darted forward, pressed his lips at the corner of Kerwin's mouth, then leaned back, too flustered to look at him. "You can call yourself whatever you want. I don't care what people think when they hear we're mates. The people who matter will know we're not bonded yet."

Kerwin's eyes widened. "Right. Jamison knows I'm your mate, doesn't he?"

"I told him yesterday after you left the coffee shop. It was the only way I could think of to get him to understand why I needed to contact you."

"I don't have a problem with him or anyone else knowing. I'm not planning on hiding us, Fergus. I'm not planning on hiding *you*."

The words almost made Fergus cry. He hadn't known what to expect from Kerwin, but now he knew he couldn't have a better mate.

He'd do everything he could to cherish Kerwin and the bond they shared. He knew he'd fuck up sometimes, and he hoped Kerwin would forgive him when he did. He wanted their relationship to work, and he was ready to do anything he could to ensure it did.

Kerwin sighed. "I should probably go back to training. My best friend will also worry if he doesn't see me."

"Of course. I'm sorry if I took you away from your job."

Fergus didn't ask what Kerwin did here. It was a secret that not even Jamison had told him, and he didn't want to get Kerwin in trouble. He was fine with not knowing, anyway.

Kerwin smiled again. He had a great smile, one Fergus wanted to see every day for the rest of his life. "Honestly, I was happy to see you. I like training, but it's harsh." He got to his feet. "I really need to go. Give me your phone number, and I'll call you once I'm done."

Fergus couldn't have done it any quicker. He barely waited for Kerwin to get his phone out before he rattled out his number. Kerwin seemed amused, but Fergus didn't care. He wanted his mate to like him, and it seemed that Kerwin did, especially when he leaned closer and smacked a kiss on Fergus's lips.

"I'll see you soon," he promised. He paused, then winked. "Mate."

Fergus watched Kerwin open the door and leave the office. He'd stood when Kerwin did, but his legs felt like jelly, so he stumbled back toward the chairs. He flopped into one, trying to get his breathing back to normal.

Holy shit. He'd met his mate, and Kerwin was the most beautiful man in the world while also being kind and gentle and nice. He was everything Fergus could have wanted, and he wanted to be with Fergus.

Was Fergus dreaming?

A knock made him look up. Jamison hovered by the open door, but he quickly came in when he saw he had Fergus's attention. "How did it go?"

"Much better than I ever could have expected."

Jamison relaxed. "Yeah? I saw him go back to training, but I didn't dare ask him."

"He wants to date me. He's not ready to bond, but neither am I, and I didn't expect him to be. I'm fine dating."

Jamison smiled. "That's great. I'm happy you found him.

You couldn't have asked for a better man."

Fergus was very much aware of that.

CHAPTER THREE

For once, Kerwin was looking forward to seeing his mother. He couldn't wait to tell her and his dad about Fergus because he was happy he had a mate, and because it meant his mother would finally stop hounding him to go on blind dates and marry a woman. She wouldn't be able to ignore that Kerwin was Fergus's mate, which sounded damn good.

It had only been a few days, but Kerwin was already organizing his life thinking of Fergus. They both had jobs and somewhat demanding families, so it wasn't easy for them to find time to be together, but they made it work by using their phones a lot. Kerwin didn't mind. He suspected Fergus didn't, either, and that he was more comfortable getting to know him through texts and silly cat pictures. It helped keep some distance between them that Fergus seemed to need.

Kerwin suspected it had to do with Fergus's family. Fergus hadn't told him much about them yet, but he didn't need to in order for Kerwin to see they were a problem. What little Fergus *had* told him had made that obvious, and Kerwin hoped he'd never have to meet them. If Fergus needed his support when it came to them, though, he'd have it.

No one should be treated like they didn't matter.

That was one of the reasons Kerwin had made it a point to tell Fergus he'd tell his parents about him. He didn't want Fergus to think he'd keep them a secret, because he had no intention of doing so. He was nervous, but there were laws about bonds and mates, and his mother wouldn't be able to ignore them, no matter what she thought of the council.

She kept ranting about the people on the council and how they didn't have demons' best interests at heart, even when Kerwin pointed out there was a demon representative on the council. She could easily ignore things that didn't fit her narrative, and he'd stopped trying to make her see otherwise. It wouldn't work, anyway. When she convinced herself of something, nothing could change her mind, even when it was obvious she was wrong.

He'd called ahead, so he knew his father wouldn't be there. He was out of town, and Kerwin wondered if that was because he was trying to stay away from his mother. He wouldn't be surprised. He loved his mother, but she could be a lot sometimes, and he could only imagine how bad it was for his father. Unfortunately, it meant Kerwin would have to tell him about Fergus on the phone, but they could see each other as soon as his father was back.

Going home to the small town where he'd grown up always made him shiver, and not just because it was still hidden under a magic blanket, which meant that only the demons who lived there could see it. He thought it was stupid, but he wasn't the one making decisions for the town. Shifters and the supernatural world in general had been out for decades now, so it didn't make sense for the demons to keep on hiding, but they seemed to want to do so, and Kerwin couldn't complain, because he didn't live here anymore. He'd left as soon as he could, even though his mother had tried to convince him not to, and he'd never regretted it.

He still didn't, and he doubted he ever would.

He drove to the big house where he'd grown up. It had been too big even back then, and he'd always wondered if his parents had hoped to have more children. He'd grown up an only child, and maybe having a brother or sister would have helped his mother not obsess over him and his future so much. He'd never find out, so it was pointless to think about it, but as he got out of his car, he wondered how his parents Felt, living on their own in this place. He supposed his father spent more time at work than at the house, so it wasn't as bad for him, but what about his mother? Maybe she was lonely, and that was why she was trying so hard to get Kerwin to marry someone. Maybe she was afraid he'd be lonely, too.

Or maybe she was just pissed he never did what she wanted him to do. Anything was possible with her.

He climbed the stone steps to the front door and knocked. Like always, it took his mother a few minutes to open. When she did, she gave him a tight smile.

She wore a white shirt, a row of pearls, and a black pencil skirt. She was very proper.

Kerwin was still in his uniform. He'd known it would annoy her, and he'd only had classroom lessons that day, so it wasn't like he was sweaty or anything like that. He'd wanted to get this over with as soon as possible, and he still did.

"I hope you're here to apologize," she said as she moved deeper inside the house.

Kerwin followed her after closing the door. "I don't have anything to apologize for, so no."

She huffed. "I think you have a lot to apologize for. I organized a wonderful date for you, and you didn't even sit with Maribel. What was wrong with her? Her family is powerful and rich, and she's a beautiful woman. She wants to get married and have children soon. She was the perfect woman for you."

Kerwin had to resist the urge to roll his eyes. "I'm sure she's the perfect woman for someone, but you seem to forget I don't like women that way."

Like every other time he'd said it, his mother ignored him. "If you're not here to apologize, then why are you?"

This wasn't going the way Kerwin had hoped it would, but he wasn't surprised. "I met someone," he said, flopping down on the couch.

His mother was annoyed at how he was sitting—which was why he'd done it—but she didn't scold him, instead focusing on what he'd said. "What do you mean?" she asked as she sat down in her favorite armchair.

"That day at the coffee shop, when I was supposed to meet you for coffee but instead found Maribel in your place? I met a guy. His name is Fergus, and he's a shifter." Kerwin sat up straighter. "He told me I'm his mate. I'm a shifter's mate."

His mother stared at him for a moment. He was almost giddy over the fact that he'd shocked her into silence. Unfortunately, it didn't last long.

His mother sniffed. "Well, that will be easy enough to ignore, since demons don't have mates and don't feel the bond."

Kerwin blinked. "What do you mean?"

"You can't possibly believe he was telling you the truth. Any shifter could tell you that you're their mate, and you can't check if it's true or not."

Kerwin almost groaned. Had he really believed this would go well? Was he an idiot? He was used to dealing with his mother, and he knew how she was when it came to his future. She was happy to steamroll him and forge ahead, ignoring anything he said or did. He'd refused to even sit down with Maribel, but he had no doubt his mother was already thinking about someone else she could throw in his arms to see if she stuck.

Kerwin swallowed and took out his phone. He pulled up a picture Fergus had sent him, even though he'd been uncomfortable. Kerwin hadn't forced him to do so, but he'd mentioned he'd like to have a picture of him, and he'd been staring at it way too often since he'd gotten it. It was probably a little creepy, but Fergus didn't know about it, and besides, they were mates. It made sense for Kerwin to be attracted to Fergus and want to look at him, right?

He turned his phone and leaned forward. "This is Fergus. He's a pigeon shifter and my mate."

Kerwin's mother barely glanced at it. As soon as she did, she looked away again, as if the sight of Fergus had offended her.

"He's not even good-looking," she said. "It won't be a problem to ignore him. Unless, of course, he's one of those people who cling on when they think they've found someone. You didn't lead him on, did you? Why do you have a picture of him, anyway?"

Kerwin sucked in a breath. It hurt when his mother didn't listen to him and went against his wishes, but it hurt even more for her to dismiss Fergus this way and insult him. Kerwin wouldn't stand for that. He'd hoped his mother would finally see the light and that she'd want to be in his life and for him to be happy, but he'd been wrong, and it was time to do something about it.

He got to his feet, startling her. She pressed a hand against her chest, dramatic as always.

"I don't want to ever hear you disparage Fergus that way. He's a beautiful man, and I'm his mate. That means something to me, even though it doesn't to you. But either you can accept this and welcome him, or you end up alone with no children. Is that what you want?"

"You can't be serious."

"I'm very serious. You need to butt out of my life and let me live it the way I want. I'm done with this. Unless you accept Fergus, you need to stay away from me."

He didn't stay to find out how she reacted. He didn't need to. He turned around and stomped away, making sure to slam the front door, even though it was childish.

Sometimes he wondered why he even bothered. Right now, he wasn't sure of the answer, and maybe he should remember that the next time she tried contacting him and forcing him into the arms of a woman he'd never met before and could never love.

Fergus was still at work when he got a phone call from his grandmother. He was always happy to hear from her, so he didn't hesitate to answer. His boss wouldn't mind, anyway. "Hey," he said.

He'd been smiling so much more since he'd met Kerwin. He couldn't wait to tell his grandmother about him, but he was a bit wary about how his mother and sister would react to the news that he'd found his mate. They'd be stunned, but even more than that, they'd have a hard time believing that Kerwin was Fergus's mate once they met him. Kerwin was too beautiful, and they wouldn't see past that. Fergus did, so he could tell Kerwin was a protector and a good person. He'd always been gentle with Fergus, and more importantly, he'd been honest. He'd told Fergus what he wanted and what he was ready for, and he hadn't expected Fergus to go along with whatever he was saying. Fergus's opinion was important to him as much as his opinion was important to Fergus.

Fergus had never thought he'd find something like that, but he was so happy he had that he'd been walking around smiling like an idiot. He'd avoided going home to his family because he'd known they'd see something was up, and he hadn't been ready to tell them. He couldn't wait to tell his grandmother, and maybe it was time.

"Fergus? Are you still at work?" his grandmother asked.

She sounded stressed, which wasn't a surprise considering who she lived with. "I am, but not for long. Did you need me to do something for you?"

"No. Your sister is in the hospital."

That firmly pushed Fergus's attention away from daydreams of Kerwin. "How is she? Is it the baby?"

"It is. She's been in the hospital since last night, but your mother didn't even think of waking me up."

Fergus could hear how annoyed his grandmother was. They both knew Fergus's sister wouldn't be a good mother and that they might have to get involved. Fergus wasn't sure it would be possible or if there was anything he could do at all, but he'd try. He wouldn't allow his mother and sister to ruin the baby before he even had a chance.

"Do you know if the baby is here?"

"He is. I was going to take a taxi to the hospital, but your mother told me not to bother and that Emily would be home soon, anyway. When I asked about the baby, she told me to forget about him."

Fergus his stomach churned. "Why? What happened to the baby?"

"I don't know. I want to go to the hospital, but I'm afraid of what I'll find there. I should be braver, but do you think *you* could go?"

"Of course." He wouldn't be doing it just for his grandmother. He wanted to know what had happened, too.

As far as Fergus knew, the baby was perfectly fine. Emily had made sure everyone knew that she was already a good mother because her baby was healthy, which had made Fergus roll his eyes so hard they hurt. Had something happened during birth?

"I really hope that baby is all right," his grandmother whispered.

"I'll go right away and let you know as soon as I can. They didn't say anything at all?"

"She just gave me the impression that they won't be coming home with the baby. I can't let them hurt him, Fergus. Please."

"Don't worry. I'll do everything I can to make sure he's all right." Although there might not be anything Fergus could do. He'd try, though.

He had to.

He quickly hung up, found his boss to explain what had happened, then rushed out. He checked his phone on his way to his car, not one bit surprised not to see a text or missed call. Whatever was happening, his mother and sister didn't want him to find out about it. They were hiding something.

He broke the speed limit on his way to the hospital, but thankfully, no cop appeared to stop him. He parked in the parking lot, took a deep breath that smelled of car exhaust, and made his way inside.

It took him a moment to find the right floor, then the right ward, but he eventually ended up in the maternity ward. A woman was walking up and down the hallway, huffing and clutching her stomach, and he could hear another one screaming nearby. It made him wince, and even though he didn't like his sister much, he hoped they'd given her painkillers.

He approached one of the nurses at the counter. "Hi. I'm here to see my sister."

The nurse smiled at him. "What's her name?"

"Emily Warrick. I was told she went into labor during the night. I realize it might not be visiting hours, but I'd like to make sure she's all right."

The nurse's expression did an interesting thing, her lips twisting from her smile to a grimace, then back. "Miss Warrick has given birth," she confirmed. She hesitated. "I normally wouldn't let you go in, but I'm hoping you can talk some sense into her."

So something *had* happened. Fergus's stomach felt like lead, and he was afraid to ask. "I've never been able to make her do anything she didn't want, but I can certainly try."

"Room eight-one-one."

He thanked the nurse with a nod, took a moment to get his bearings, then headed toward the room the nurse had indicated. He walked past the pacing woman and nodded at her, but she was too busy to notice him.

He had a hard time thinking of his sister as a mother. She was irresponsible and immature, but hopefully, giving birth would help her grow.

It didn't sound like it had.

The door of the room was open when he reached it. He knocked and peeked in, ignored the women stretched out in the other beds, and made a beeline for Emily, who was in the bed by the window, their mother sitting in a chair next to her.

They both glared when they saw him, but it wasn't enough to stop him. If something had happened to the baby, he wanted to know.

"Grandma called me," he said when he stopped by his sister's bed. "She said she wanted to come but that you told her not to bother. What happened? How's the baby?"

His mother snorted. "You can go see him if you really want to."

"Why isn't he here? What happened?" Fergus was done playing games. Normally, he'd go along with it because he didn't want to fight, but not this time. It was too important.

"I still can't believe a filthy demon took advantage of your sister," his mother spat out. "That baby won't be coming anywhere with us."

Fergus frowned. "Took advantage? Emily, what's she talking about?" She'd never mentioned knowing who the father was, having been assaulted, or anything like that.

She refused to look at him, focusing on her hands instead. "It's like Mom said. I'm sure he took advantage of me, because I would never sleep with a demon."

"I don't care who you won't sleep with. What happened to your *son*?"

"He's not her son," their mother snapped. "We'll be going home tomorrow, and the baby will stay here. I don't care what happens to it."

Fergus took a step back, horrified. He'd known his mother was a monster, but he'd never expected her to abandon his sister's son. She'd been looking forward to spoiling him as much as she spoiled Emily and had been boasting about becoming a grandmother.

He looked at Emily, and his stomach sank when he saw she was nodding.

"You can't possibly be thinking about abandoning your son." He had to find a way to change her mind.

"I don't want to raise a demon," she protested.

"And I won't allow her to," their mother said. "As far as I'm concerned, she never had a son."

They didn't want the baby just because he had a demon father? Fergus's mouth tasted bitter. "That baby needs parents. Why does it matter that he's half demon?"

"No child of mine will have a demon baby."

Fergus stood up straighter. "No? Yet one child of yours has a demon mate."

He hadn't meant to tell his mother about this today or like this, but he was done hiding.

If his sister didn't want her baby, he'd take him.

Kerwin almost didn't take out his phone when it rang, fearing his mother was trying to contact him. He'd left the house in a huff, and he had no intention of talking to her anytime soon, but he wouldn't be surprised if she tried to make him feel guilty for what he'd said and, of course, for the fact that he was planning on being with Fergus.

But it wasn't her. Fergus's picture was on the screen, and Kerwin quickly stepped out into the hallway. He was back at the facility where he and the other trainees worked and lived, and since he shared a room with several of them, he didn't want them to overhear the conversation. Wallace was the only one he'd be comfortable with, because they were friends.

"Hey," he said, already smiling as he answered.

"I need help," Fergus blurted out.

He sounded panicked, which alarmed Kerwin. "What happened? Are you all right?"

"I'm fine, at least physically."

Kerwin could hear people talking on Fergus's side of the phone, but he couldn't hear what they were saying. Fergus was supposed to be at home, so what was going on that he sounded like he was freaking out so badly?

"Take a deep breath and tell me what's happening," Kerwin ordered.

Kerwin sucked in a breath as he waited for Fergus to be ready to talk to him. He really hoped that whatever had happened wasn't a disaster. It was bad enough that he had to deal with his mother and her reaction to their relationship.

Maybe that was what had happened. Fergus had mentioned he'd tell his family about Kerwin eventually, but from the way he'd said it, Kerwin hadn't thought it would be anytime soon. Besides, even if they were angry and had yelled at Fergus, it wasn't a good reason for him to be panicked.

"My sister gave birth." Fergus sounded breathless.

He'd told Kerwin that his sister was pregnant and that it was a complicated situation, but that was all. Kerwin had no idea what else there was to it, and he didn't know enough to be able to comfort Fergus right now. "Is she all right? And the baby?" If something had happened to her, it would make sense for Fergus to be freaking out.

"She's fine. They're both fine, but she doesn't want him."

Kerwin blinked. He hadn't expected that. "She wants to leave her baby at the hospital?"

"Yes. I don't know if she wants to, but my mother convinced her to do just that."

"Why don't you tell me everything? I'm a bit confused, but I want to help."

"My sister has never known who the father was. She and my mother said it didn't matter, and I suppose it wouldn't have, except for the fact that the baby's father is clearly a demon."

Kerwin leaned against the wall. What were the odds that Fergus had a demon mate and that his nephew was half-demon? "What's the problem with the baby being half demon?"

"My mother, well, she doesn't like demons or anyone who doesn't look human. My sister kept telling her the father had to be a shifter, but she was wrong, and now they both refuse to have anything to do with the baby. I even told them about you because I hoped it would help change their mind, but it didn't."

If Fergus's mother hated demons, she wouldn't want anything to do with her grandson. She also probably wouldn't want anything to do with Fergus if he decided to be with Kerwin, which made Kerwin wonder where they stood.

"So they're not taking the baby home," Kerwin said, to make sure he understood things correctly.

"They're not. When I told my mother about you, she laughed, then told me that if I'm a demon lover, I could take the baby." Fergus paused, then continued. "I want to."

Kerwin wasn't surprised. As soon as Fergus had explained his sister didn't want her son, Kerwin had known this would happen. Family was important to Fergus, and it hurt him that his family was so awful. He wouldn't want the baby to pay for that, and he'd want to give the little boy the best life he could.

"Okay, let me talk to one of the trainers. It's getting late, and they don't like us being out at this time of the evening, but I'm sure that if I explain that my mate's sister has just given birth, they'll make an exception. I'll come to you, and we'll talk things out."

Because if Fergus decided to take in this baby, he wouldn't be the only one involved. Kerwin supposed Fergus could give up on the bond between them if Kerwin wasn't okay with adopting the child, but he wasn't sure he could do that. He didn't want to lose Fergus. He didn't want to hurt Fergus that way or abandon him when he needed him the most.

But he was only twenty-four. He was training to become a council assassin. His life didn't have space for a child, or at least he didn't think so.

He'd find out soon enough.

"Thank you." Fergus sounded relieved. "I'm not sure what to do, and I'll be relieved to have you here."

"Don't worry about anything. I'll ask a friend to shimmer me to you so I don't have to drive. That way, I'll be there faster."

"I'm not going anywhere," Fergus promised.

Kerwin wondered if when he reached his mate, it would be to find Fergus holding a baby. Even if it was, it wouldn't be the worst thing in the world.

It also wouldn't be the easiest one to deal with.

Kerwin hung up even though he didn't want to and went to look for the trainers. He found them gathered in the break room, talking and drinking beer. When they heard him, Jamison jumped up and quickly joined him, leaving the others behind.

"What is it?" he asked.

Kerwin stared. "Fergus didn't call you?"

"No. Was he supposed to?" Jamison frowned. "Has something happened?"

"His sister gave birth, and apparently, she won't keep the baby because he's half demon."

Jamison swore. "Damn her and their mother. Let me guess. Fergus won't leave the baby behind."

"I don't know what he'll do, but he called me in a panic and needs me there. Can I go?"

Jamison didn't hesitate. He nodded, clearly aware how much his best friend needed them. "Go, and tell him I'll come by soon, too. He'll need all the support he can get to face his family." Jamison stared at Kerwin for a moment. "I don't know how much Fergus told you about his family, but if you're about to meet them, I should warn you they're assholes. Well, Fergus's grandmother is a sweetheart, but his mother and sister are spoiled brats who pitch tantrums if they don't get what they want and are cruel to Fergus. He'll need you if he's going to face them, and you need to know what will be in front of you."

"I'll be there for him," Kerwin promised.

"Good. Now go. I'll tell the others what's going on."

Kerwin hadn't told anyone except Wallace that he'd met his mate, but everyone would know by the time he came back. He didn't care. He hadn't told them because it was new, and he wasn't close to all the other trainees, but he wanted them to know he and Fergus were together.

For better or worse, even though they weren't married.

He quickly went back to his room to change, told Wallace what was happening, then got one of the other trainees to shimmer him to the hospital. He'd either go home with Fergus once this was over or catch a shimmer through one of the apps he had on his phone. How he got out of the hospital didn't matter — the only thing that did was to get there.

Kerwin rushed inside. It took him a moment to find the maternity ward, and he couldn't ignore how many people were staring at him. Once he got to the ward, though, things got strange. The nurse at the counter gave him a room number without even having to ask, and he hoped it was the room where Fergus was waiting.

Before he could head that way, the nurse spoke again.

"Your brother-in-law is with the baby right now," she said.

Kerwin blinked, then realized what had happened. He was a demon, and the baby was half-demon, so the nurse had assumed he was the father. It was strange, but it meant he'd be let in, which was all he wanted. "Thank you."

She nodded, her expression grim. "Good luck."

He followed the signs toward the nursery instead of going to the room, since he wouldn't find Fergus there. He doubted there were many demon babies in the nursery, so he'd know which one was Fergus's nephew, and he was curious.

He didn't have to wonder which baby it was.

When he got there and peeked through the window, he found Fergus sitting in a corner, a blanket-wrapped bundle against his chest. Fergus hadn't seen Kerwin yet because he was staring at the baby in his arms.

The baby looked like he belonged there, while Fergus looked like a father.

Fergus stared down at the baby in his arms. How could Emily not want him? He was beautiful and perfectly healthy, and the way he looked, with the light green swirls on his skin and his tiny tail, only made him more precious. Fergus couldn't let him go.

Which meant he'd have to make a choice. He and Kerwin had never discussed having children, but they'd only known each other for a few days. It had been too soon to have that kind of conversation. Fergus was scared, though. Kerwin was only twenty-four, and he'd only recently started training for a job that would end up being dangerous. Would he want the burden of having a child?

What would Fergus do, then? Could he choose between his nephew and his mate? He might have to, and even though his heart broke, he already knew which way he'd go if that was the case. He wanted to give his nephew a good life, and if he had to give up his mate to make that happen, he would. He was ready to sacrifice a lot for this baby, who he already loved, even though it didn't make sense.

The baby didn't even have a name yet. Emily had refused to name him, and while the nurse had asked Fergus to do so, he hadn't been able to bring himself to yet. He had hope that even with everything going on in Kerwin's life, he'd want to take on this, too. If he did, they'd raise the baby as parents, which meant Kerwin should have a say in the name.

A gentle knock on the window made him look up. He was relieved to see Kerwin there, smiling at him. Kerwin's gaze drifted down to the baby, and Fergus gently moved him until Kerwin could see his face. He was sleeping, so Kerwin couldn't see his swirling eyes, but he could probably imagine them. The baby had a shock of light green curly hair poking from the small hat on his head that had made Fergus smile when he'd first seen it. He'd never thought about babies until Emily had gotten pregnant, but for some reason, he hadn't imagined they were born with so much hair.

As gently as he could, he went to put the baby back in the bassinet. The nurse nodded at him when he left, and as soon as the door was closed behind him, he threw himself into Kerwin's arms. He was afraid Kerwin would push him away, and he sobbed in relief when instead, he wrapped his arms around him and held him close. Fergus clung to him, unable to stand facing this on his own anymore.

"It's fine," Kerwin whispered. "Everything is fine. I'm here now."

Fergus nodded and took a step back. He dried his eyes with the sleeve of his sweater, then looked up at Kerwin. "For how long?"

"As long as you need me. Why don't we go see your sister? You can give me more details about what's been happening on the way, and hopefully, we'll manage to change her mind."

Fergus already knew they couldn't. "She won't change her mind. She's already planning on going on vacation next week with her friends. My mother is paying for it." He sucked in a breath. "They tried to make *me* pay for it, but I told them to fuck off. It's the first time I can remember ever talking to either of them that way."

Kerwin wrapped an arm around Fergus's shoulders and squeezed. "I'm proud of you."

Fergus nodded. He still had to call his grandma, but she'd agree with Kerwin.

But now he had to face Kerwin and how complicated their situation had become. "You know, I'll understand if you want to take a step back," he said, doing just that and putting more distance between him and Kerwin. "You never signed up for this. You just found out you have a mate, and I can't burden you with a child, too."

He could feel Kerwin staring at him, but he was afraid to look up. What would Kerwin's reaction be? Anyone in their right mind would run out of the room as fast as they could. Kerwin didn't need to be involved in this. He didn't need to become a father.

"Did you know that the nurse assumed I was the baby's father when I came in?"

"I can see it. You're more of a yellow-green, while he's light green, but I guess you *could* be his father."

"I could be his father and your mate, and we could be a family."

Fergus shook his head. "It's too much to ask. You don't need this kind of responsibility."

"I'm not saying I don't have doubts or that I'm not wondering how we'll make it work, but I'm not leaving you to do this alone. We're mates."

"Yes, but you don't feel the bond as strongly as I do. It shouldn't be a problem for you to take a step back. Even if you don't want to do it permanently, we could be apart for the next, I don't know, ten years? Maybe eighteen. I'd wait for you."

Kerwin grabbed Fergus's arm. "I don't want you to wait for me. It wouldn't be fair for me to ask it of you, and I'm not going to. I'm also not going to abandon you. You're not alone, Fergus."

Fergus almost cried. He allowed Kerwin to pull him against his chest again. They stayed there, snuggled against each other until a baby started crying. Fergus instantly pushed away to check if it was *his* baby, but the boy was peacefully sleeping.

"You're already so much a father," Kerwin murmured. "Now come on. Let's talk to your mother and sister. The sooner we get that out of the way, the sooner you can come back to your son."

There was no way to know if Fergus would be allowed to take the baby. He'd started thinking about what it would take for him to be allowed, and he got a headache. He needed to contact a lawyer, but he had no idea where to start.

Thankfully, Kerwin seemed to know, or maybe he'd already started researching before reaching the hospital.

"We need to get your sister to talk to a lawyer so she can sign off her parental rights," he said as they walked along the hallways. "I don't think there's anything that would go against you taking in the baby. It'd be better for him to be with you than go into the foster system, right?"

"I don't know. Where am I supposed to find a lawyer?" And how was he supposed to pay for one?

"I'm pretty sure the council has a list of lawyers happy to work with shifters. We'll be able to find someone there." Kerwin took his phone out of his jeans pocket and started typing.

"I'm texting Jamison."

"How do you have his number?"

"We all have the trainers' numbers. He can look into this while we deal with your family."

Fergus really wasn't alone. He hadn't realized it before, but he couldn't ignore it now, and it lifted a weight off his shoulders. "I have to warn you that they won't be happy to see you. They, well, they don't like demons, and they were disgusted when I told them about you." But Fergus didn't care if it meant he could take the baby. That was all he wanted to focus on.

Kerwin had taken control, and Fergus was happy to surrender. After texting Jamison, Kerwin started making a list of things they needed to buy for the baby. Fergus would have to take time off work, but his boss was nice, so it shouldn't be a problem. Besides, he hoped he could request paternity leave. That was a thing, right?

Fergus's life would be a whirlwind in the next few days, especially once the baby was allowed to leave the hospital, but he could do this.

He didn't have a choice.

CHAPTER FOUR

Kerwin didn't know how to help Fergus. Jamison had taken things in hand, finding a lawyer and dealing with the official side of this mess, and Fergus had been spending a lot of time at the hospital with the baby. Kerwin had, too, and since he'd told the trainers what had happened, they hadn't had a problem with it. He felt he could do more, but he wasn't sure what.

He was an adult, but barely. He hadn't thought he'd have to deal with having a baby for years, possibly decades, and while it was fairly easy to get used to the fact that he had a mate, the baby was more complicated. Kerwin needed help, and there were only a few people he could think of that could give him that.

He just hoped his mother wouldn't ruin everything.

She hadn't always been the way she was now. Kerwin wouldn't say she'd ever been a loving mother, not the way he'd seen some of his friends' mothers be, but she'd been nice when he was growing up. She changed after he became an adult, sometime in the past couple of years. It had gotten worse last year when he'd applied to become an enforcer. She'd been pissed and had tried to change his mind, and she didn't even know about the assassins' training for which Kerwin had been privately contacted. He was glad she didn't know what he was actually doing, but since then, she'd started trying to force him into things he didn't want. She wanted him to change his life, and he wasn't willing to do that.

But right now, he needed his mother. Hopefully, she'd understand that and let go of whatever resentment and anger she still had over what he was doing. Besides, she was a mother. She'd gone through what Fergus was going through once, and since Fergus wouldn't be getting any help from his own mother, Kerwin's was their last hope.

He still wasn't convinced this was a good idea.

After checking in with Fergus and making sure he didn't need anything before they met at the hospital, Kerwin drove to the village where he'd grown up. His mother wasn't expecting him, but he hadn't called her on purpose. He wanted to surprise her to see her real reaction to what he'd tell her. If he gave her too much time, she'd be able to hide how she felt, and he needed to know where they stood.

Even though the baby wasn't technically Kerwin's, he was giving his mother what she wanted, right? She wanted him to find a partner and have children, which was precisely what he'd done. Fergus might not be the kind of partner Kerwin's mother wanted for him, but he was the kind of person *Kerwin* wanted. She'd have to learn to deal with that, and Kerwin prayed the baby would distract her.

That didn't stop him from being nervous. He wanted to turn his car around as soon as he parked in front of the house, but instead, he steeled himself and walked up to the front door. He knocked, then listened to the sound of his mother's footsteps coming closer. She wore heels even in the house, which had always struck Kerwin as uncomfortable. If his mother couldn't be comfortable in her own home, where could she be? Maybe that was why she was always so angry.

The door opened. Today, Kerwin's mother wore black pants with her usual white shirt. Her hair was arranged in a low bun at the back of her head, and her tail was tightly wrapped around her waist.

"Kerwin," she said, blinking at him. "What are you doing

here?"

"I need to talk to you."

Her eyes narrowed. "Have you come to your senses?"

It took Kerwin a moment to understand what she was talking about. "You mean about my mate?"

She pressed her lips together. "It doesn't matter if he's telling the truth and he really is your mate when you're a demon. You don't have to be with him."

Kerwin sighed. He didn't want to fight, although he could admit that his mother's reaction to seeing him didn't bode well. "Can I come in?"

"Of course."

She stepped aside, and he followed her through the house. It was the middle of the day, so his father was at work, which was a pity. He'd be happy to find out he had a grandson. Kerwin hadn't wanted to ruin the news for his dad, though, which was why he'd decided to talk to his mother alone. That way, if she exploded, he'd be the only one hurt in the process.

"If you're not here to tell me you've decided to give up that shifter, why did you come?" she asked as soon as they were in the living room.

"You see, Fergus's sister just had a baby. He's half demon, which means she doesn't want to keep him."

"Please tell me you didn't volunteer to raise that child," Kerwin's mother snapped.

This *definitely* wasn't going the way Kerwin had hoped. "I didn't, but Fergus did, which means that both of us will raise him."

Kerwin's mother pressed a hand over her heart. He couldn't remember ever shocking her like this, which was a giddy feeling. He might have grinned if it wasn't clear she was angry enough to explode. She'd never raised a hand to him, but that didn't mean she couldn't do damage.

"Why are you doing this to me?" she asked.

"I'm not doing anything to you. I'm doing what I feel is right and what I want. It's my life, after all."

"And you're ruining it. You're settling down with a shifter and a bastard child. What do you think will happen? It'll ruin your chances to have a good wife and your own children."

Why had Fergus hoped his mother would change her mind? He should have known better. She'd been against Fergus from the first time Kerwin had mentioned him, and while Kerwin had hoped that having a baby would help her accept Fergus, it was clear that she didn't want her grandchildren to come from just anywhere. She didn't believe that Fergus's nephew could be Kerwin's son. They weren't related by blood, which meant she'd never consider the baby part of her family.

Kerwin stood up straighter. He'd always intended to be by Fergus's side to help him through whatever happened next, but his mother's reaction made it easier to accept.

Kerwin's mother was still talking. "This will make that man cling to you even harder. Don't you see? He needs you more than he did before and more than you need him. He'll never let you go, and you can't afford for that to happen. You need to step away, and you need to do it before he does something stupid like biting you without your consent."

Kerwin hadn't sat down, and he was glad, because it meant he could leave as soon as he wanted. He didn't like what his mother was saying, though, and he wouldn't be shy telling her that. "Don't talk about Fergus that way. He's not clinging to me. If anything, he tried sacrificing himself by telling me I could step away. He told me he'd raise the baby on his own and that we could reconnect once the baby was an adult. He'd never bite me without asking first, and besides, I'd have to drink his blood, too, to complete the bond."

"Good. Let him think that. By the time the child is grown, you'll have your own kids and wife, and he'll be nothing more than a memory."

Had she heard anything Kerwin had said? He'd come hoping to save his relationship with his mother, but now, he wondered if there was anything he could do or say to make that happen. He'd been willing to make compromises, but she was still bent on him marrying a woman she'd handpick for him and having children with her. She'd never accept Fergus or Fergus's nephew, no matter how much Kerwin had hoped she would.

He turned toward the door. He was done with this. He was done with his mother, and right now, if he never saw her again, he'd be happy. Unfortunately, she was still married to his father, so he'd have to come back, but he'd deal with that when he had to.

"Where are you going?" his mother called out.

She didn't come after him because it would have been unbecoming of a woman like her. Kerwin almost laughed at the image of her rushing through the hallway, trying not to run as she came up to him. He couldn't hear her heels, though, so he knew he was safe.

He turned, stopping in the middle of the hallway and staring at her. "I'm leaving. I'm going back to my mate and our son."

"Don't you dare do that," she snapped. "I'll never talk to you again if you do. This isn't what I want for you."

"But it's what I want for myself, and that's the only thing that matters. I hope that eventually, you'll be able to accept my mate and your grandson. In the meantime, don't call me. I don't want anything to do with you."

"Kerwin!"

But Kerwin was done. His mate and their son were waiting for him, and that was the only place he wanted to be.

"Are you sure they won't try to stop us?" Fergus asked Jamison.

Jamison quickly squeezed Fergus's arm. "They can't. The social worker went over all the documents, and as long as your sister signs the paperwork to give up her parental rights, your nephew will go home with you today."

The thought was terrifying, but Fergus had gotten used to it. It had only taken a few days to get everything in place, which had surprised him until he realized Jamison had used his job for the council and the people he knew there to help speed things up.

Today, Fergus's sister was leaving the hospital. From what he'd heard, she was already planning everything she'd pack to go on her vacation, and as far as he knew, she hadn't mentioned her son even once. She'd given birth to him, then had forgotten about him and moved on.

Fergus didn't hate her for that. It didn't even surprise him now that he'd had time to think about it. He didn't think it was hatred, at least not from Emily. After all, she hadn't cared enough not to sleep with the baby's father. Being a mother was too much for her, though, and their mother's hatred for demons gave her the perfect opportunity to get out of the situation. By doing what their mother wanted and giving up the baby, she was also giving up the responsibility of being a mother, which was all she wanted.

Fergus couldn't say he was sorry. He'd been shocked, and he'd tried to change her mind, even though he'd known he wouldn't be able to. This was for the best, anyway. She wouldn't have been a good mother. She wouldn't have been abusive, but Fergus wasn't convinced their mother wouldn't have been. It was a pity the child would never have grandparents, but he'd have parents who loved him, and that was all that mattered.

"What will you call him?" Jamison asked as he, Fergus, and

the council lawyer walked into the hospital.

The woman was kind of scary. Kendra German had a no-nonsense attitude. Sometimes she stared at Fergus as if she were trying to read his mind. After he'd explained what had happened the first time they'd met, she'd stared at him that way and asked what he intended to do. She'd seemed satisfied with his answer that he was planning on becoming the baby's father, and she'd put all of it in motion.

And now, Fergus was here to pick up his baby.

He groaned at Jamison's question. "We haven't decided yet."

Jamison chuckled. "You're going to have to choose a name eventually. You can't keep on calling him *baby*."

Fergus bumped their shoulders together. "I'm aware. We haven't really had a lot of time to talk." Fergus had been dealing with his mother and sister, his grandmother, his job, and buying everything he'd need for the baby. His apartment was too small, but it would have to do until he managed to find a bigger one. It wasn't like the baby would need space for the first few months, anyway.

Kerwin had been there with Fergus every step of the way. He couldn't focus only on Fergus, though. He had his job, and he'd decided to try talking to his mother again. Fergus had never met her, but considering what he'd heard of her, he wasn't in a rush to. If anything, he wanted to keep her as far away from his baby as he could. But she was Kerwin's mother, and it made sense that he'd wanted to talk to her one last time. For his sake, Fergus hoped he'd be able to change her mind.

He suspected it would take a miracle, though.

"Tell me," Jamison said.

Fergus bit his lower lip. "I like Theodore."

Jamison thought it over for a moment. "It's nice, and it goes well with your surname. Or is he taking Kerwin's name?"

"He's taking mine."

"I like it. Theo for short?"

"Yeah."

"Why don't you text Kerwin and ask him if that's okay with him? If he agrees, you can fill in the paperwork and take Theo home by the end of this visit."

Fergus had hoped for that, since the baby was healthy and ready to go, and the excitement made his stomach churn. He might not have any idea what he was doing, but he knew what he wanted.

To take Theo home.

But first, they needed to talk to Emily, so that was where they headed. Fergus wasn't surprised to see that her bags were already packed. She and her mother were talking and behaving as if Emily had never had a baby. They both turned when Fergus knocked on the door, and while Emily seemed hesitant, their mother was clearly pissed.

"What are you doing here?" she asked. "If you're going to try to convince your sister to take that baby, you can stop. We're leaving him here."

Kendra made a hissing sound behind Fergus, and he quickly stepped in. He was pretty sure Kendra might try to beat up his mother with her messenger bag if she continued talking about Theo like he didn't matter.

"I'm not expecting you to do anything when it comes to the baby," he quickly explained. "Since Emily doesn't want him, I need her to sign away her parental rights."

Emily blinked. "I can't just leave him here?"

She sounded so young right now that it hurt Fergus's heart. When he thought about it, she *was* extremely young. She was twelve years younger than him, and she'd barely started her life at twenty-three. She was technically an adult, but with the way their mother had raised her, she'd never gotten the chance to mature.

"My name is Kendra German," Kendra interjected, pushing Fergus away. "I'm Fergus's lawyer, and I have the documents to sign away your parental rights. I also have documents that attest that you want your son to be adopted by your brother."

"You're keeping him?" Emily asked.

She sounded curious and maybe a little hopeful. Maybe she'd never meant any harm to the baby and just didn't want him.

"You can't adopt him," their mother snapped. "He's half demon."

"And I seem to remember you telling me that since I was a demon lover, I should take him. That's what I'm planning to do. My mate and I will raise him."

"You're still going on with that nonsense? You can't have met your mate."

That hurt, no matter how many times his mother had said it. "Well, I have. I'd have introduced him to you if you hadn't been such a bitch."

His mother hissed and moved toward him, but Jamison blocked her. He was big, with broad shoulders, and Fergus's mother didn't dare push past him.

Kendra cleared her throat. She kept her focus on Emily, who was staring at the papers she was now holding.

"There are X's where you need to sign," Kendra explained. "It's for the best."

Emily licked her lips. "Why would you want to do this?" she asked Fergus.

"Because that baby didn't do anything to deserve to be abandoned. I'm not blaming you for not being ready to be a mother. I'm ready to be a father, though."

Emily nodded, took the pen Kendra was holding out to her, and quickly walked to the nightstand. Their mother tried to stop her, but once again, Jamison was there, glaring down at her.

"If you sign those papers, your brother won't care about us anymore," their mother said. "He'll be focused on that little monster, and we won't see him again. And think of the money."

It was partially true. Fergus had no intention of taking his son to visit his mother, but his grandmother still lived there. They'd have to do something about that, but Fergus could only focus on Theo for now.

Emily shrugged. "I don't need him. Besides, I'm sure that if I do, he'll come back."

The dismissal hurt, but Fergus was relieved when his sister signed all the papers. It was what he'd wanted and what he'd hoped for, and for once, things had gone his way.

It would take time for him to become Theo's father. The council would have to process all these documents, but thankfully, Theo was a supernatural creature, so the council would take care of it. They were much faster than the human justice system, and all of that meant that Fergus could take his son home right now.

When his sister pushed the documents back into Kendra's hands, Kendra quickly went over them. As soon as she was done, she nodded at Fergus.

It was official. Fergus had become Theo's father.

Kerwin was still fuming as he drove away from the house where he'd grown up. He was so angry that he wasn't thinking straight, so as soon as he felt he was far enough away, he stopped the car in the first parking spot he could find. He quickly texted Fergus to check in on him, smiling when his mate answered that his sister had signed all the documents and that he'd be taking their son home as soon as the hospital was okay with it.

It would take a while longer for everything to be official, especially if Kerwin wanted to adopt the baby, but this was what Fergus wanted, and while Kerwin was more hesitant, he wouldn't have done anything differently. He couldn't say he'd expected to become a father at twenty-four, and he knew it wouldn't be easy, but he was ready.

He smiled at the picture Jamison had just texted him of Fergus holding their son. Jamison had even teased Kerwin that he hadn't been there to choose the baby's name, but Kerwin and Fergus had talked about it. Kerwin had known the name Fergus preferred, and he quite liked Theo, too, so he didn't have a problem with it. He should have been there to support Fergus, but Fergus had insisted he try talking to his mother again when he'd mentioned he might, and they'd wanted to avoid a confrontation with Fergus's family. Kerwin was glad he'd be there when the baby was released from the hospital, and he'd drive Fergus and Theo to Fergus's apartment. Kerwin had already talked to the trainers, and he had the next few days off from training so they could learn how to be a family. He'd be there for Kerwin, no matter how hard it was.

But he still had someone to talk to, so he quickly pulled up his father's number and called. He wasn't surprised when his father didn't answer. He was at work, and even when he wasn't, he usually forgot where he'd put his phone. Hell, he often forgot to charge it, so it was a small miracle that it was ringing.

Kerwin could imagine what his father would go home to tonight, and he wanted to warn him. His mother could say whatever she wanted, but the only truth was the one Kerwin would provide.

Since he couldn't talk to his father, he texted him. It took way too long to put what he wanted to say into words. He'd already told his father he'd met his mate, and his dad had been happy. He'd wanted to meet Fergus, and that was before

Theo had come into the picture. He'd be even happier now, or at least, Kerwin hoped so. The fact that he wasn't sure was the only reason he hadn't told his father about the baby yet. After the way his mother had reacted, he was terrified his father would push him away, too. A shifter mate seemed to be all right, but would a half-shifter, half-demon baby be okay, too?

Kerwin would find out eventually. After sending his text, he started the car again and aimed it toward the hospital. He wanted to get there as soon as possible, but he made sure not to go over the speed limit.

It was a relief when he reached the parking lot. He climbed out of his car and was almost to the front door when it opened, revealing a young woman. She was talking to someone slightly behind her, complaining about the way her body looked.

"I'm never getting pregnant again," she said with a whine.

"You're certainly never getting pregnant with another demon spawn. I'm thinking about suing the people who did your ultrasounds. How did they not see the tail?" an older woman said, following the younger one outside.

Kerwin stepped aside to let them pass. They both looked up, and the older woman's expression shifted to disgust. Kerwin held her gaze. It could be a coincidence, but he was pretty sure he knew who these women were. He had no intention of introducing himself to them.

Or maybe he should. After what had happened with his mother, he was in the mood to annoy someone.

He beamed at the woman. He didn't even know her name, and he didn't care. "Hello."

"Let's go," the woman said, grabbing her daughter's arm and pulling her away, dragging both her and a rolling suitcase.

"It was a pleasure to meet you, mother-in-law," Kerwin

called out behind her.

Her back stiffened, and she slowed down just enough to glare back at him. He didn't expect her to do anything and certainly not to talk to him, so he turned and headed into the hospital. That had been fun and made him feel a little better, but it was time to focus on what was important.

His mate and their son.

Jamison had been keeping Kerwin updated, so he knew he'd find Fergus and Theo in the nursery. That was where he headed, feeling nervous until he finally saw both of them.

Fergus was holding Theo against his chest as he listened to what a nurse was saying, nodding along to her words. Jamison stood beside him, with a woman Kerwin recognized as the lawyer Fergus had been using to get the paperwork in order. She and Jamison were softly talking, and Kerwin barely nodded at them before going to stand next to Fergus.

Both Fergus and the nurse turned to look at him when he arrived. Fergus smiled, but Kerwin could see he was a bit nervous. That wasn't surprising, and it mirrored the way Kerwin felt, but together, they could get through this and anything else life threw at them. Kerwin would remind Fergus about that, even if he had to do so time and time again.

"We all have a soft spot for Theo," the nurse said, looking from Fergus to Kerwin. "And everyone is glad he'll have a loving family."

Fergus and Kerwin looked at each other. Kerwin didn't care how hard it would be. He was in this for life.

"Thank you for everything you've done," Fergus said to the nurse as he looked back at her.

"You take care of that baby."

She stepped away, and Kerwin wondered if that was it. "Can we take him home to your apartment?" he asked Fergus.

"We can. Kendra took care of all the paperwork."

"Not all of it," Kendra intervened. "There will be more

paperwork for the adoption, but your sister gave up her parental rights, and the council authorized you to take Theo home. For now, you're his guardian. Once the adoption papers go through, you'll officially be his father. I don't think anyone will attempt to fight it, but paperwork always takes time. In the meantime, you can start settling down and being a family."

"That's the plan," Kerwin said as he wrapped an arm around Fergus's waist.

He peered down at the baby. Theo was asleep, and while it wasn't the first time Kerwin saw him up close, like the other times, he was surprised at how much they looked like each other. He truly could have been Theo's father.

Theo's face was a bit squashed, but Kerwin had been told that was normal for newborns. It didn't take away from the light green swirls on Theo's skin, or the tiny tail that Kerwin knew was hidden under the blanket Theo was wrapped in. He also knew that when Theo opened his eyes, they swirled black and light green. The nurses had cooed about that every time he was awake. Kerwin had expected the color, but clearly, there weren't many demon babies born in this hospital.

That wasn't surprising. Even though the supernatural world had been out to humans for more than twenty years now, demons tended to keep to themselves. They stuck to the villages where they'd hidden before the world had found out about them, and most of them never came out. They liked their lives to be traditional, which was one of the reasons Kerwin's mother was so bent on him marrying someone from their village and moving back.

But Kerwin had left the village, and he'd never been happier. He was glad he wasn't stuck there anymore and that he could explore the world, although that might be a bit hard with a baby.

They'd make it work. He and Fergus were young, and they'd still be once Theo was an adult. They had all the time in the world to do whatever they wanted later. For now, they needed to become the best parents Theo could have.

And that was what Kerwin was planning on doing.

"I only have one question left," Kendra said, looking from Fergus to Kerwin.

Fergus wanted the questions to be over. He needed to get Theo home, and it was becoming harder to ignore that need. It was like an itch under his skin, almost as if he was afraid that if he didn't take Theo away, someone would try stealing him.

"What is it?" he asked cautiously.

"I'm going to file the adoption papers as soon as I'm done here. Your name is on them, of course, but what about Kerwin?"

Fergus blinked, taking a moment to understand what Kendra was talking about. "You mean you want to know if Kerwin wants to adopt Theo, too?"

She nodded. "The two of you are mates, so it's technically not needed. The council will consider both of you Theo's fathers as long as you bond eventually. I would normally suggest this if you weren't mates, but you are, so it's not like either of you is going anywhere, but some people want to have both parents on the paperwork to make things easier in case something happens."

It was a possibility but not something Fergus wanted to think about. He turned to Kerwin. "What do you think?"

Kerwin stared at him and Theo for a moment before nodding. "He's going to call me Dad anyway, and Kendra is right. I'm not going anywhere. The two of you are it for me for the rest of my life. Having my name on the adoption papers will make it official in case it's needed, and I want to have all bases covered."

Fergus had known they were going to do this together, but it was a relief to hear the words. He couldn't stop himself from smiling, especially as he glanced at Kendra and saw how satisfied she looked. She knew what she was doing.

"I have a few things for you to sign, then," she told Kerwin. She gestured at him to come closer, and he obeyed.

He clearly wanted out of this hospital as much as Fergus. The sooner they dealt with the paperwork, the sooner they'd be home.

Well, at Fergus's apartment. It wasn't home for Kerwin, who lived in the facility where he worked. He hadn't officially moved in with Fergus yet, and Fergus didn't know if he'd be allowed, but they'd have to talk about it. Not today, though. Today, he wanted to focus on the baby in his arms and on the family they were forming. Everything had gone too quickly, and Fergus had felt completely lost more than a few times. He still did, but what he was doing was right, which was enough for him to be able to deal with whatever the future would throw at them.

By the time they were done signing all of Kendra's paperwork and the hospital's and were finally ready to go, Fergus was tired. He kept expecting Theo to wake up, but the baby had stayed asleep against his chest so far. He'd never dealt with a baby before, but he was pretty sure that wouldn't last for much longer, which meant they needed to get home.

"Do you need anything else?" Jamison asked as he walked Fergus, Theo, and Kerwin to Kerwin's car.

"We'll be fine," Fergus promised.

Jamison didn't look convinced. "Have you ever taken care of a baby?"

"No, but neither have you. You heard the nurse. She told me everything I needed to know and showed me how to change his diaper. I can do this." Or at least, Fergus hoped so.

Because even if he realized he couldn't do this, it wasn't like he could take Theo back. He'd signed the papers, and Theo was his responsibility now. He didn't regret it, but he couldn't deny he was terrified about what would come next.

It took him a moment to understand how to buckle Theo in his car seat. He was sweating by the time he was done, but Jamison stopped him when he tried walking around the car to the passenger seat.

"What?" Fergus asked. Kerwin was already in the driver's seat, waiting for him to climb in.

"I'd suggest you sit in the back with the baby. What if he wakes up?"

Fergus bit his lower lip. He hadn't thought of that. How could he not have? "Thank you."

Jamison smiled. "Any time, and I mean that. I'm just a phone call or text away if you and Kerwin need anything. Call me, even if it's because you need a nap."

"You've never taken care of a baby," Fergus pointed out again.

"I'll learn with you and Kerwin."

It was a reminder that Fergus wasn't alone in facing this. He'd always known he'd have Kerwin, but it wasn't only him. Jamison was there, too, and between the three of them, Fergus was pretty sure they could raise Theo to be a good man.

Like Jamison had suggested, Fergus climbed into the back seat next to Theo. He waved goodbye to Jamison, then leaned his head against the seat and closed his eyes.

"Everything okay?" Kerwin asked.

"Better now," Fergus promised as he looked down.

Theo's eyes blinked open. Fergus held his breath, wondering what Theo would do.

He started crying.

Fergus knew better than to take Theo out of his car seat, so he tried to calm him as best he could. Thankfully, his apartment wasn't far, but by the time Kerwin parked in front of the building, Fergus's ears rang. Theo hadn't stopped crying the entire time, and Fergus had no idea what he needed. As soon as the car stopped, he rushed out of his seat and walked around the car, grabbing the newborn. He needed to check his diaper and see if Theo wanted to eat. Beyond that, he had no idea what else he could do, so he hoped one of those would work.

He rushed into the apartment, leaving Kerwin to grab the few things they needed from the car. Fergus had set up a changing table in the corner of the living room, and he headed there first. He changed Theo's diaper more easily than he'd expected, but by the time he was done, he was exhausted. Theo had quieted some, but he still whimpered every so often, and Fergus tried to soothe him by holding him against his chest and walking around the living room.

"It was the diaper?" Kerwin asked.

"I think? Gosh, I don't know what I'm doing. I'll be a shit father because I can't even tell what my son needs."

Kerwin gestured at Fergus to hand over Theo. Fergus liked having Theo in his arms, but he let him go because it meant he could get a bottle ready.

"You're not a shit father," Kerwin said as he cradled Theo against his chest. "You're a new father, and I don't think any new parent knows what they're doing except if they've already had babies in the past. You're doing everything you can, and you're doing a good job."

"Yeah?" Fergus needed that reassurance.

"I promise. We'll figure this out together, all right?"

And they did. Kerwin hovered next to Fergus as Fergus got a bottle already. Fergus did everything the nurse had covered and followed the formula's instructions. He even made sure the milk wasn't too warm before handing the bottle to

Kerwin, who took it with a satisfied smile.

While Kerwin fed Theo, Fergus went to the bathroom and splashed some water on his face. He had to remind himself that he wasn't doing this alone and that he'd make mistakes. Every parent did, and no matter how bad he was at this, he couldn't be as bad as his mother. She'd been a shit parent, and as long as Fergus did the opposite of what she'd done, he'd be better.

Telling himself that made him feel better, and by the time Theo was done with his bottle and ready for bed, Fergus felt calmer. He'd had his first freak-out, and he'd worked through it with Kerwin's help. Maybe there was some truth to the saying that mates found each other when they needed it the most. Fergus would have been entirely lost if he hadn't had Kerwin by his side through this, but thankfully, he did. He'd met Kerwin at the perfect moment in his life, even though he hadn't known it that day in the coffee shop.

"All right?" Kerwin asked as he flopped onto the couch next to Fergus.

The house was blissfully silent, a sure sign that Theo was sleeping—for now. Fergus twisted to look at him, folding a leg under his body. He stared at Kerwin for a moment, and Kerwin stared back.

"Thank you." The words were both easy and hard to say.

"You don't have anything to thank me for," Kerwin said.

"I do. I don't think I'd be able to do this without you. So, thank you. Thank you for not running away as soon as you realized how complicated this would be. Thank you for being patient with me. Thank you for taking on the role of father even though you didn't expect to become one anytime soon."

Kerwin cupped Fergus's cheek and gently kissed him. "If you're thanking me for all of this, then I should thank you for giving me something I never thought I'd have."

"A surprise baby?"

Kerwin laughed. "That, too. But no. I meant you. I wasn't supposed to have a mate, but I can't imagine life without you."

Fergus didn't want him to, and as he kissed Kerwin again, he promised himself he'd do everything he could to make his mate happy. They weren't just parents. They were mates, and Fergus would cherish Kerwin as much as he cherished Theo.

CHAPTER FIVE

W hen Kerwin's phone rang, he threw himself toward it. He'd forgotten to put it on silent, and he'd throw it out the window if it woke up Theo, who Fergus had just managed to convince to fall asleep. Kerwin was tempted to tell whoever was calling to go to hell, at least until he saw it was his father.

They still hadn't talked, and he was anxious. He was afraid of what his father would say about Theo, especially since his mother had had time to get to him. Normally, Kerwin's father didn't listen to her. He hadn't when it came to Fergus, and Kerwin knew his parents had fought over that, but they were still together. That meant his father loved his mother, right?

Kerwin almost snorted. He wasn't naïve. There were many reasons for his parents to still be together, and most didn't have anything to do with love. Right now, he couldn't understand how anyone could love his mother, but he realized it was because he was angry at her.

"Hello?" he answered. He peeked toward the bedroom, but he couldn't hear any noise coming from it.

"Kerwin, did I catch you in a bad moment?" Kerwin's father asked.

"The baby just fell asleep, but I don't think he woke up."

There was a moment of silence. Kerwin held his breath, not knowing what to expect.

"I know you texted me to tell me about this, but it's incredible to hear you talk about a baby," his father eventually said.

Kerwin snickered and relaxed against the couch. "It's even more incredible to have to change his diaper and feed him."

And to watch him grow day by day. Kerwin was smitten.

"I bet it is. I remember when you were little. You were so small that I was afraid I'd hurt you."

Kerwin had felt the same way with Theo the first few days, but he was more confident now. Even though Theo was tiny, he wasn't as breakable as Kerwin had expected, which was good. Kerwin wasn't planning to drop Theo or anything like that, but it made him feel better about learning how to be a father.

"Theo is great," Kerwin said cautiously. His father sounded happy, but there might still be more behind all of this.

"I'd like to meet him, if it's at all possible. I know your mother didn't take the news well, so I'd understand if you'd rather keep your distance."

"I'll be honest. I want you and Theo to get to know each other, and I want Theo to have at least one grandparent, but I'm afraid of how she'll react. I won't put my son in danger."

"I can't make promises when it comes to her behavior. You know your mother. She doesn't do or say anything she doesn't want, and she won't allow anyone to silence her."

"That's why I haven't introduced her to my mate. She was so rude when I told her about him and showed her his picture."

Kerwin's father sighed. "I understand. I just wanted to reassure you that I'm thrilled to become a grandfather."

Kerwin hesitated. He wanted Theo to meet his father, even though the baby wouldn't remember it. Kerwin's dad would, though, and this was the best moment to start their relationship. If Kerwin wanted Theo to grow up with his grandfather in his life, it would be better to start right away, especially since Kerwin's father was willing and even happy to do so.

Kerwin also wanted Fergus to meet his dad. They both had rotten luck with their families except for his dad, and it didn't feel right to keep him away just because of Kerwin's mother.

But Kerwin was unwilling to expose his mate and their son to his mother's sharp tongue. She'd never raise a hand to them, but she could do a lot of damage with her words. Theo might not understand them, but Fergus would.

Kerwin chewed on his lower lip, trying to find a way to make this happen. "Maybe we could meet away from the house?"

"That would be a good idea, and I can't wait, but I believe that first, we should have a conversation as a family."

That was the last thing Kerwin wanted. "You mean the three of us?"

"Yes. Your mother's behavior since you met your mate and even before has been appalling. I knew it, and I feel guilty about not doing something sooner. I told myself that you're an adult and could deal with it, but I was wrong. Your age doesn't matter. The only thing that does is that you're my son, and I should have protected you, even if it was from your mother."

Kerwin couldn't say he disagreed about either of those things. His father should have intervened sooner, but Kerwin also should have stood up to his mother. He'd needed to meet Fergus to realize that and to finally stand up for himself, but his father was right. They needed to talk, and maybe, with him there, Kerwin and his mother would manage to smooth things out. Kerwin doubted they could ever have an easy relationship considering what she'd put him through recently, but surely, they could be civil to each other at the very least. He wouldn't be able to avoid her if he wanted a relationship with his father. Besides, maybe a conversation would finally break through whatever hatred she had for how Kerwin lived his life.

"I'm only giving her one last chance," Kerwin warned.

"It's one more than she deserves, and I'll make sure she

doesn't hurt you."

"She can't anymore. I know what to expect, so I won't be surprised by anything that comes out of her mouth. Are you home right now?" Because as far as Kerwin was concerned, the sooner they got this out of the way, the better it would be.

"I'm home, so you can come now if you want."

"Let me check with Fergus. I don't want to leave him alone with the baby, so I'll also call a friend. I'll let you know, all right?"

"I'll be waiting at home."

Kerwin would be going, if anything, because he missed his dad. Maybe now that they were clearing things up his father would start spending less time at work and more time at home, and Kerwin would be able to see him more often. His father hadn't exactly been an absentee dad when Kerwin was younger, but he also hadn't been very present. It would be nice to see if things could be different with Theo.

After they hung up, Kerwin peeked in on Fergus and Theo. Theo was in his crib while Fergus had stretched out on the bed. He sat up as soon as he noticed Kerwin, but Kerwin went over and gently pushed him back down. "It was my father," he murmured.

"Oh?" Fergus's body had tensed, no doubt because he didn't know what to expect from Kerwin's father.

Kerwin hadn't, either, but he was relieved now that he'd talked to him. "He wants to see me. He's happy about Theo, and he can't wait to meet him, but he thinks we should first have one last conversation with my mother. I think he's going to try to change her mind."

"Do you think he'll succeed?"

"I want to say yes, but I doubt it. Honestly, I'm done with her. After the things she said about you and Theo, I don't think I'll be able to make peace with her even if she apologizes. We'll see, though. I don't want to close off that opportunity just yet."

"At least your father is on our side."

"He is." Kerwin pressed a hand on the mattress and leaned forward to kiss Fergus's forehead. "I'm going to head over there right now. I'll call Wallace before leaving. He'll be happy to come over and help you with Theo."

"I don't need help with Theo."

"You don't need to need help to ask for it. You know Wallace wants to be Theo's favorite uncle." He'd fallen in love with the baby at first sight, and he hadn't stopped talking about him since.

It was nice to have someone excited about Theo in Kerwin's life, which was why Kerwin was happy to get Wallace to spend as much time with Theo as possible. Wallace was as clueless as they'd been when it came to taking care of a baby, but he'd taken to it like a duck to water.

Fergus pressed his forehead against Kerwin's forearm. "I feel like you and I haven't been spending enough time as a couple, even though we've been together almost the entire time since Theo got out of the hospital."

That much was true, but most of their time together was spent focused on the baby. Kerwin loved it, and he loved Theo, but he couldn't wait to have some adult time with Fergus. He felt like they were losing their relationship a little, and while there wasn't much they could do about it right now, he promised himself he'd find a babysitter so that he and Fergus could go on a date. They'd still been trying to find their way to each other when Theo had come into the picture, and it would do their relationship and them a lot of good to be alone for an evening.

But first, Kerwin had to deal with his mother one last time.

Fergus wished he'd been able to go with Kerwin, but Kerwin

would have said no if he'd offered. He'd been keeping Fergus away from his mother, which was a good thing considering what Fergus knew about her.

But it made Fergus feel as if he wasn't supporting his mate. The bond between them had gotten a little lost since they'd brought Theo home, and Fergus wasn't quite sure how to hold onto it.

Shifters who'd just met their mates spent several weeks, if not months, attached to their mate's hip. It was the draw of the bond, but also getting to know each other and starting a relationship. Even now, he didn't like being away from Kerwin, and his pigeon was pushing at him to go to their mate. It was pushing for a lot of things these days, though, so it was easy to ignore it. Fergus felt the need to shift like an itch under his skin, and he knew that soon, he'd have to give in and fly, but for now, he needed to keep an eye on Theo.

He wasn't alone in the apartment. Wallace had arrived about fifteen minutes after Kerwin had left, way too excited for an afternoon of babysitting. Fergus didn't know Wallace well yet, but he liked him, and he could see Wallace becoming a friend and part of his family. He already was part of Kerwin's, and considering how bad the situation was with their actual blood families, it was good to have people who cared.

"You should try taking a nap," Wallace suggested from the couch.

Fergus had moved to the living room when Wallace had arrived so he wouldn't be left alone, but things had been a bit awkward between them. He sat in his armchair while Wallace was on the couch, and both of them were silent. Wallace kept peeking at Fergus, and Fergus wondered what it was about. Maybe Wallace had a question and wasn't sure whether or not he should ask it. At this point, Fergus wished he would because it was becoming more awkward as time passed.

Maybe the nap thing was what he'd been trying to say. He

could have been afraid that Fergus would be offended at his insinuation that he looked tired, but Fergus *was* exhausted. Waking up every two or three hours every night was taking a toll, even though Kerwin tried to help as much as he could.

Fergus forced himself to smile. "I'm fine."

"If you're worried about Theo, you don't have to. I know how to deal with him now."

"I know you do, and I'm glad for the help, but you didn't need to come."

The corner of Wallace's lips curled. "Kerwin was being overprotective?"

"A bit. I mean, I don't know how long he'll be out, but even if it's for the rest of the day, it wouldn't be a problem. I don't have anywhere to go, and I can take care of Theo." Fergus's boss had given him paternity leave, just like Fergus had expected. Fergus realized how lucky he was with his job, and he had no intention of ever quitting, but he would have for Theo. Theo's mother had abandoned him, but Fergus wouldn't.

Of course, he wasn't sure how he'd have kept Theo fed if he'd had to quit his job, but luckily, that wasn't something he needed to worry about.

"He cares about you," Wallace said.

"I know."

Wallace nodded. "And he's a good guy. I don't think I have to tell you that, considering the situation, but he truly wants both you and Theo in his life. He wouldn't be here otherwise."

"I never doubted that." Fergus had known there was a good chance Kerwin would want him, if anything, because they were mates. Even though Kerwin was a demon, he could feel the pull of the bond, albeit not as strongly as he did.

"We were all surprised when he told us about you, but in a good way. If there's one person who deserves a mate, it's Kerwin."

"We don't choose our mates, but I'd have chosen him,"

Fergus murmured.

Wallace beamed at him. "Good. He's head over heels for you, although I realize it might be hard for you guys to do something about it with the baby." Wallace leaned forward. "You know what you should do? Take him out on a date. I could babysit Theo for a few hours, and you and Kerwin would have time to be together. I'm not blaming you for this mess, but I'm sure both of you could do with some time away from Theo and the responsibilities that come with him."

Wallace was right. Fergus did want to go on a date with Kerwin, but he also panicked at the thought of leaving Theo behind, even though he knew his son would be safe. Wallace was trustworthy, and it wasn't like Emily would try getting her son back. She'd signed the paperwork and had made her decision, and even if, by some miracle, she wanted to see Theo, she'd never want the responsibilities that came with him. Theo was Fergus's son now, and no one could take that away from either of them.

Fergus smiled, finally relaxing. "I think we'll take you up on that."

Wallace beamed. "Good. I've always wanted to work with kids, and I love spending time with Theo."

Fergus blinked. "Why *aren't* you working with kids?"

He knew a little more about what Kerwin and Wallace did at the training facility now. Well, he knew they were training to become part of a special secret team that would work exclusively for the council, but he was afraid to ask questions. Kerwin had given him a few details, and he'd even hinted that the team wouldn't always do things the legal way. It would be dangerous and maybe not the best job, since Kerwin was a father now, but Fergus wouldn't try to stop him. Kerwin had gone into this training knowing what he was signing up for, and as long as he was careful, Fergus would accept it.

But this stuff didn't sound like something Wallace was

comfortable with, especially now that he'd confessed he wanted to work with children. Wallace's expression also told Fergus a lot, and he hoped he hadn't touched a delicate nerve with his question.

"My father got me the spot on the team," Wallace explained. "All the men in my family work for the government. Well, they work for humans, since they've been at this a lot longer, but now it's my turn, and my father managed to get me this job. He was extremely proud when I passed all the tests."

"Did he ask you if this was what you wanted?"

Wallace snorted. "My father doesn't ask. He orders my brothers and me to do something, and we do it because we won't like the consequences if we don't."

Fergus's heart broke. He was saying this as if it was a given, as if it was normal for his father to behave as if he and his brothers were nothing more than soldiers.

Fergus would never treat Theo that way. Theo would be allowed to do what he wanted with his life, and Fergus would support him every step of the way, whether he wanted to be a clown or an astronaut. It didn't matter to Fergus as long as he was happy.

Even though clowns were creepy.

Wallace smiled. "You won't do this to Theo."

"Never," Fergus promised. He couldn't help Wallace, but he could make sure Theo had the best life possible. "But I understand where you stand. My mother and my sister aren't good people. They're cruel and always were, but I clung on until Theo happened. After he was born, I couldn't allow them to hurt him the way they hurt me. I had to let them go, and it was easier than I expected."

Wallace slowly nodded. "It's something I've been thinking about. I'm not sure what to do yet, but maybe you're right. Maybe it is time for me to take a step away from my father and the rest of my family."

"You have to live your life, not theirs." And even though life would inevitably surprise him the way it had surprised Fergus, Fergus had no doubt that, eventually, Wallace would find his way to happiness.

Kerwin was nervous every time he came home. At least this time, he knew he'd have his father's support, and it helped him keep his head high as he climbed the stone steps to the front door and knocked.

He waited and listened for his mother's footsteps, but he didn't hear them. When the door swung open, his father welcomed him, beaming at him as if Kerwin was the most incredible thing he'd seen all day.

Maybe he was.

Kerwin's father opened his arms, and Kerwin threw himself into them. They wrapped around him, holding him close and reminding him that through all of this, he'd never been alone, even though he hadn't realized it.

"It's so good to see you," Kerwin's father murmured.

"I missed you," Kerwin answered.

"I missed you, too, and I promise that from now on, I'll dial down on my work and spend more time with you. You have a family now, and I want to be part of it."

Kerwin took a step back, rubbed his prickling eyes, and stared at his father. "I wish we didn't have to do this." Kerwin was happy now, and he didn't want to fight with his mother.

His father sighed and closed the door. "I know, but we need to nip this in the bud. I don't want your mother to think she can dictate your life and, even worse, that she can ask you to give up your son."

"I don't think she considers him my son." In fact, Kerwin was sure of that.

"Whether she does or not, that baby is yours, and it won't change. She needs to accept it or take a step back from this family."

Kerwin sucked in a breath. He hadn't expected his father to choose him over his mother, but maybe he should have. His father had always supported him, even when he'd spent long days at work. He hadn't known about the blind dates and pushing Kerwin to marry a nice local girl, but that was because Kerwin had never told him. He hadn't thought he needed help dealing with his mother, and he still didn't.

Things had changed when he'd met Fergus. Kerwin had refused to go along with his mother's plans then, and that was when she'd turned mean. He'd stopped being her puppet and had dug his heels in, which wasn't what she was used to. He'd wanted to keep the peace before and had been unwilling to deal with the headache he had to deal with now, but not anymore.

Never again.

His father sighed. "I didn't tell your mother you were coming, but I'm sure she heard the knock. She'll know someone is here, and she'll come looking. We might as well go to her."

"I guess we don't have a choice." Kerwin was here to do this, even though he didn't want to. Once this conversation was over, they'd all know where they stood, and hopefully, it would be easier for him to move forward.

Kerwin followed his father to the kitchen. His mother didn't cook — she hired someone to do it for her — but she enjoyed sitting at the breakfast nook in the afternoon. Sure enough, that was where they found her.

She looked up when she heard them. Her eyes widened, and she focused on Kerwin's father. "What is he doing here?" she asked, ignoring Kerwin.

Things were not off to a great start.

Kerwin's father clearly wasn't impressed. He crossed his

arms over his chest and glared.

Kerwin's mother glared right back.

"He's your son," Kerwin's father said. "And this is his home. He can visit whenever he wants, with or without his mate and their son."

Kerwin's mother got to her feet. "Kerwin doesn't have a son."

And there it was. Once again, Kerwin was both unsurprised and disappointed. He'd known there was only a slim chance for his mother to change her mind, but hearing her talk about Theo as if he was nothing hurt and made Kerwin angry. Theo was just a baby, and he deserved to be loved, not rejected.

Kerwin's father stood up straighter. His expression was thunderous, and Kerwin sucked in a breath. He didn't think he'd ever seen his father like this.

"You'll stop treating our son like he doesn't know what he's doing. You'll stop trying to force him into relationships he never wanted. I can't force you to accept Fergus and Theo, but I can make sure you'll never say anything disparaging about them ever again," Kerwin's father said.

Kerwin's mother opened her mouth. Her eyes blazed with anger, and Kerwin was tempted to take a step back. He couldn't remember ever seeing his parents fight, and he was stunned.

"No," his father snapped, interrupting his mother before she could say anything. "I've allowed you to hurt my son for too long, but not anymore. If you insist on pushing me, I'll make you regret it."

"You'll *make me regret it*? What do you think you can do?" Kerwin's mother asked.

Kerwin's father smiled, but it wasn't a nice smile. "I'm the only provider. I pay for the house, the food, your car, and all your trinkets. What do you think will happen to you if I decide to ask for a divorce?"

Kerwin's mother took a step back and reached for the table to hold herself up. Kerwin was as shocked as she looked. He'd never expected his father to threaten divorce. He couldn't believe what he'd just heard.

"You wouldn't," Kerwin's mother whispered.

Kerwin knew it would hurt her, and not only financially. Kerwin's family was wealthy, but if his father divorced his mother, she might have to find a job. She wouldn't be able to keep up with her friends, but then, she'd probably be too ashamed to want to see them again. Her reputation was more important to her than her son. She'd never do anything to put it in jeopardy.

"I would," his father promised. "I've allowed you to hurt Kerwin for too long. It was easy to ignore it when I was working all the time, but I decided to cut down my hours. I'll still see my patients, but I won't take any new ones, at least for a while. I want to be part of my son's and grandson's lives. It's fine if you can't accept that, but I won't listen to you say anything nasty about either of them."

Kerwin's mother looked from his father to him. Everyone in the room knew she'd lost, including her, so it wasn't a surprise when instead of fighting back, she huffed and strode out of the room. She didn't look back at Kerwin or say goodbye to him, and he wondered if they'd ever talk again. He was fine with the answer being no. He didn't want anything to do with her if she behaved this way.

"Thank you," he told his father.

"You have nothing to thank me for. I should have done this long ago, when you were still a child. I'm sorry that because of me, we didn't spend as much time together as we should have, but I'm ready to do whatever I can to fix that. It won't be the same since you're an adult now, but as long as I can have a relationship with you, I'll be happy."

Kerwin dragged his father into a tight hug. "I *am* happy."

He wasn't sure how things would work between them, but they'd find a way. Even though his father had been somewhat distant, he'd always been there for Kerwin, and that was all Kerwin cared about. He'd never demanded Kerwin do things the way he wanted like Kerwin's mother had, and as far as Kerwin was concerned, his father had always been the better parent between the two of them. He'd made mistakes, but Kerwin had no doubt he and Fergus would make them with Theo.

"I can't believe you threatened her with a divorce," he said once they separated.

"It wasn't just a threat. To be honest, I've been thinking about it more and more lately. It made sense for us to stay together while you were still a child and living with us, but you're an adult now. You have your own life, and I'm sure you can understand why I might want out of this marriage. I'll confess that the main reason I stayed was that it was easier, but not anymore. Not if she hurts you."

"She won't hurt me again."

"Damn right, she won't. I suppose we'll see what the future brings." He looked Kerwin straight in the eyes. "I'm proud of you."

Kerwin was old enough that he shouldn't have felt so happy about that, but this was still his father. "Thank you."

"You have a good job with the council, a mate, and a child. You're living your life without compromises, and it's something I admire. I wasn't able to do that when I was your age."

Because his marriage to Kerwin's mother had been arranged by their parents. Both of them had gone through with it, and Kerwin was starting to suspect that his father had been miserable all these years.

Not anymore.

"You can find all of this, too," he promised as he hugged

his father again.

"I hope so, Kerwin. Now, tell me about your mate and your son."

Kerwin was happy to do just that.

Fergus had been worried about Kerwin and how his visit with his parents was going. After what Kerwin had told him about his mother and her reaction to the news that Kerwin was a shifter's mate, Fergus didn't expect it to go well. Kerwin still had hope, but Fergus had been through similar situations too often. He understood why Kerwin still had hope, though, and he'd prayed that everything would go well for his mate's sake.

It hadn't. Kerwin had texted Fergus a while ago, telling him that his mother had blown up but that he was talking to his father. It sounded like at least he was accepting of Kerwin having a mate and a son, but the news had left Fergus nervous.

Was this what Kerwin actually wanted? He'd never signed up for a mate, let alone a son. Fergus had been trying to do most of the work because he didn't want Kerwin to regret choosing him, but he suspected Kerwin had noticed. He always insisted on getting up during the night to change and feed Theo, and he also spent time with the baby when he came back from training. No matter how often Fergus told him to get some rest, Kerwin insisted that he was Theo's father, too, and he was right.

Fergus's instinct was to take on as much as possible because he was afraid that if it became too much work for Kerwin, he'd leave. Kerwin needed to focus on his training, because even though Fergus didn't have details about what it was for, he knew it was important, or rather, that it would be once he was done and ready to start working. Kerwin had tried telling Fergus more, and Fergus wanted to know, yet he was scared to find out at the same time. They'd both been busy, so they'd skipped that conversation for now, but it wouldn't last forever.

Fergus chewed on his bottom lip and checked his phone. He had to keep in mind that he was Kerwin's mate, which meant Kerwin wasn't going anywhere. It wasn't because of the bond, either. Kerwin was a good man, and he'd made promises he intended to keep. For some reason, he liked Fergus and wanted to be with him so much that he'd accepted that Theo would be part of their lives. He was even adopting Theo, which was one more sign he was in this for the long term. Fergus hated that because of the way his family had treated him that he was afraid to believe Kerwin, but it would take time for him to wrap his mind around that.

He would, eventually.

The sound of a key in the front door's lock made Fergus jump up from the couch. He wanted to throw himself at Kerwin, but he was afraid. He didn't know what Kerwin and his father had talked about, but considering how late it was, it had to have been good. Right?

The door opened, and Kerwin came in on silent feet. He looked around, smiling when he saw Fergus there. He closed the door quietly, and Fergus made his way to him.

They stood in front of each other. Fergus didn't know what to say, so he reached out and took Kerwin's hand. When Kerwin smiled, Fergus relaxed.

"Everything okay?" he asked in a whisper.

Kerwin's smile widened. "Yeah. I mean, my father told my mother that if she didn't stop being nasty about you and Theo, he'd divorce her, but he and I are just fine. We talked, and he apologized for not being there for me. He wants to get to know you and Theo. He wants to be a grandfather and to be in Theo's life."

Fergus relaxed. He'd thought that being with him would take everything from Kerwin, and he was glad to hear that wouldn't be the case. "So Theo will have at least one grandparent."

Kerwin nodded. "Yeah. My father isn't going anywhere."

"Good." Fergus sucked in a breath. "I'm sorry you lost your mother because of me, though. I realize it hasn't been easy for you to get used to having a mate and a son, and I wish you'd let me do more. I can take care of Theo during the night. You need rest, but I don't have anything else to do—"

Fergus was forced to shut up when Kerwin kissed him. He sucked in a breath, but he didn't push Kerwin away. He wanted nothing more than to be in Kerwin's arms, so he sank against his mate, knowing Kerwin would hold him up.

"You're doing more than enough," Kerwin whispered against Fergus's lips.

He kissed down Fergus's neck, and Fergus tilted his head back to give him more access. His body felt warm, and he wanted more, but he wasn't sure he should even ask.

He and Kerwin had been sharing a bed, and they made out every time they had a few minutes together, but that was all they'd done. Fergus wanted more, but every time they started, Theo woke up, or Kerwin got a phone call, or the alarm on Kerwin's phone went off, and he had to go to work.

None of that had happened tonight, but they might. At the very least, Theo could wake up, but Fergus had put him to bed only half an hour ago after changing and feeding him, so he and Kerwin should have at least an hour and a half, hopefully more.

"Let's go to bed," Fergus murmured.

Kerwin straightened. "Yeah? What about Theo?"

They'd placed the crib in a corner of the living room, mostly because Fergus wanted Kerwin to be able to sleep through the night without Theo waking him up. That was why they'd both been so quiet just now — Theo was sleeping in the corner.

"I just put him to bed."

"So we have a little time?"

"More than a little, hopefully."

Kerwin snickered. "Now that you said it, he's going to wake up."

They both froze and listened, but there was nothing to hear. Theo was sleeping.

Fergus grinned and took Kerwin's hand. He pulled his mate toward the bedroom, and Kerwin came without resisting. He stopped once they stepped into the bedroom, though, and for a moment, Fergus thought something was wrong. He turned, afraid of what he'd see in Kerwin's expression, but as soon as he faced him, Kerwin pulled him into his arms again and kissed him.

Then he shocked the fuck out of him.

"I want us to bond," he whispered.

Fergus blinked, sure he'd heard that wrong. "What?"

"I'm on Theo's adoption papers, and you heard Kendra. She thinks it'll make it smoother and easier if you and I are bonded."

Fergus pulled away, but Kerwin didn't let go. "You want us to bond because of Theo?" Fergus wasn't opposed, but he wanted Kerwin to want him, not just Theo. He realized he wasn't exactly a catch, but he didn't want Kerwin to eventually regret bonding with him, maybe when Theo was grown and it was just he and Fergus left.

"No. I want us to bond because I'm your mate, and I never imagined I could be this happy. I was resigned to fending off my mother's blind dates and being single for the next few years at least, and considering what I'm training for, I didn't think I'd have the possibility of a significant relationship until years from now. Instead, I have you and Theo, and I couldn't be happier. It's everything I never knew I wanted until I got it, and I'm not planning on going anywhere. Bonding with you doesn't have anything to do with Theo. I want us to be together, and I don't see a reason for us to wait. We're together, and we will be for years to come. Bonding won't change that, but it will make it official. I'll be able to tell everyone that you're mine, and that's what I want, even though I realize it makes me sound like a caveman."

It did, but Fergus liked it anyway.

Kerwin kissed Fergus's forehead. "Why don't you take some time in the bathroom? I'll be waiting for you in bed, and you can tell me what you decide."

He stepped away from Fergus, and Fergus took the out. He rushed to the bathroom, needing a moment of respite, even though he already knew his answer.

How could he say no?

He'd never wanted anything more than a mate and a family. He had so much love to give, and until now, he'd had no one to give it to. With Kerwin and Theo in his life, he was more settled and, even with the complications and difficulties, happier. They were all he wanted, and he could have them forever.

Fergus quickly showered. He didn't want to waste time in case Theo woke up, and he was thankful not to hear the baby when he stepped out of the bathroom, wearing only a towel.

He was less thankful to find Kerwin asleep.

Fergus wasn't even angry. Kerwin had to be exhausted, which was understandable.

With a sigh, he dropped his towel and slipped into bed. He snuggled close to Kerwin and pressed a hand against Kerwin's stomach, then waited to see if Kerwin reacted. The peaceful expression on Kerwin's face made him smile. Kerwin would be annoyed tomorrow morning, but sleep was more important than sex.

Fergus kissed Kerwin's cheek, then leaned back, ready to go to sleep, too, but Kerwin groaned. He wrapped one of his arms around Fergus's waist and pulled him close. He slid his hand down Fergus's waist, encountering only naked skin, and Fergus felt him freeze.

"Fergus?"

Fergus kissed Kerwin's jaw. "Go back to sleep."

"I can if that's what you want, but I'd like to know what you decided."

Fergus wouldn't have been able to go back to sleep if their roles had been reversed, so he doubted Kerwin would. And once he told Kerwin he wanted them to bond, there was no way Kerwin would want to wait.

They were doing this, and they were doing it now.

"Yes," Fergus whispered. They didn't have a lot of time, but he didn't want to rush things.

When he looked up, Kerwin's expression was tender. Fergus didn't have a better word for it, and he didn't need one. It was lovely to have someone watch him that way.

"Are you sure this is what you want?" Kerwin asked. "I won't leave you because we don't bond or because things get hard with Theo. I realize your family made it hard for you to trust me, but I'll show you that you can and that I'm not going anywhere."

Fergus frowned. "You think I'm saying yes just to make sure you won't leave?"

"I think you're afraid I will, but also that I'll regret bonding with you. You're torn because you want to bond with me, but you're afraid I'll change my mind eventually. You're also afraid of disappointing me. I just want to know what *you* want."

Fergus pressed a hand over Kerwin's heart. It was racing, telling him Kerwin was as nervous as he was. "I want you in any way I can have you. And yes, I want to bond with you.

You're my mate, and you're perfect."

Kerwin stared for a few moments as if he was trying to read Fergus's expression, and maybe he was. Whatever he saw there must have satisfied him because he smiled. "All right."

"So we're bonding?" Now it was Fergus who needed to be sure. He didn't have to tell Kerwin that if they did this, it would be forever. Kerwin knew what he was asking and clearly, what he wanted.

"Yes."

Kerwin pulled Fergus closer to kiss him. Fergus let go, the tension in his body releasing. They really were going to do this.

Kissing Kerwin was perfection, and Fergus could spend days doing just that, so when Kerwin leaned back, he tried to follow him. Kerwin chuckled and gently pushed Fergus away. Fergus was hurt until he realized it was because Kerwin was still wearing his underwear. He quickly wiggled out of it, pushing it to the bottom of the bed, then dove back on Fergus, who laughed and rolled to his back.

He liked feeling Kerwin pinning him to the mattress. In fact, he couldn't get enough of it. He opened his legs, and Kerwin settled between them as if he belonged there.

He did. His place was there, in Fergus's life and in his arms, and after tonight, he'd be there forever.

Fergus wrapped his arms around Kerwin's neck and whimpered at the feeling of their naked bodies pressed together when Kerwin lowered himself more fully. He was heavy, but not too much, and his dick was hard. It pushed into the groove between Fergus's hip and his thigh, sliding against Fergus's skin with every movement Kerwin made.

"I don't know what you had in mind," Kerwin whispered, "but I just want to be close to you."

Fergus wanted everything, but they had to consider the situation. "Maybe we can ask Wallace to babysit one day soon so we'll have more time. I'm scared Theo will wake up in the middle of this."

Kerwin chuckled, then bit Fergus's throat hard enough to sting. "That's a definite possibility. It's a pity, because I want to be able to spend time exploring and tasting you."

Kerwin thrust against Fergus. Fergus's cock rubbed against Kerwin's stomach, and Fergus's breath hitched. Fergus doubted they'd have the time, anyway. It had been a while since he'd had that kind of sex, and considering how horny he was, he'd never be ready before he came.

"Yeah, we can do that later," he breathed out.

Kerwin hooked his arms under Fergus's shoulders, locking them together. Fergus could only grab his mate's shoulders, holding on for dear life as Kerwin moved against him. Kerwin's neck was right there, ready for Fergus, and Fergus couldn't look away.

When Kerwin noticed it, he grinned and lowered his upper body closer to Fergus's, tucking his face against Fergus's neck. He bit down again, and Fergus reacted on instinct, his fangs out before he could even think about it.

They sank into Kerwin's neck, and blood spurted into Fergus's mouth.

This was what Kerwin tasted like. This was what would bond them together. It didn't taste great, but Fergus didn't care.

He lost himself in Kerwin's taste and in the way he smelled. His skin was warm, and he was still moving, chasing his pleasure and giving so much of it back to Fergus that it was overwhelming. Fergus had to close his eyes against the many sensations because there were so many of them. No one had ever loved him like Kerwin did. No one had ever treated him like he was precious.

But Kerwin did.

Fergus needed the bond to be complete. He reached for his

neck, desperately scratching at it. Kerwin caught his hand, trapped it against the mattress, and bit him again. Fergus opened his mouth to tell him he didn't have fangs when the pain hit. He almost screamed, but thankfully, he managed to stop himself in time, and instead, he drank another mouthful of blood.

He felt the bond reaching between them. It wasn't complete yet, but it would be soon.

Fergus came when it sprang into place. Everything Kerwin was feeling pushed inside of Fergus, confusing and overwhelming him. It was too much for him to be able to focus, so instead, he let go. He dragged his face away from Kerwin's neck and sucked in a breath as pleasure coursed through his body, making his limbs tremble.

He knew the moment Kerwin came, too. He could feel it, and it triggered a smaller but no less powerful orgasm in him. It was like a never-ending loop, and by the time things finally calmed down, Fergus felt like he'd run a marathon—actually, make that two.

Kerwin slumped to the side, grunting when he hit the mattress. He reached for Fergus, his fingertips sliding against Fergus's skin, his tail wrapping around one of Fergus's legs. They should clean up soon because it wouldn't be long before Theo woke up, but Fergus didn't have the energy to move.

"Theo?" Kerwin asked.

"Can't hear him right now."

Kerwin snuggled against Fergus's side. "Good."

Fergus huffed. "It won't last for long."

"That's fine. I just want a few minutes to savor this moment."

Even though they'd have the rest of their lives to savor being bonded, Fergus settled down next to Kerwin and did the same.

Which, of course, was when Theo started crying.

CHAPTER SIX

Wallace was too quiet.

Kerwin had been keeping an eye on him lately, and he'd seen his friend retreat deeper and deeper into himself. He didn't know what had caused it, but he could imagine, and he had no idea what to do about it.

He bumped their shoulders together. "Want to talk about it?" he asked, even though he suspected the answer would be no.

Wallace smiled, but it didn't reach his eyes. "Talk about what?"

"What has you so pensive."

"Kerwin, do you have something to share with the class?" Hawthorne asked from the front of the room.

Wallace's cheeks flushed and he ducked behind his book, but Kerwin grinned at the trainer. "Nope, sorry."

Hawthorn arched a brow, but thankfully, he didn't ask anything else and turned back to whatever he'd been explaining.

Kerwin should be focusing on the lesson, and he'd tried, but he was tired, and not just physically. Thankfully, things were smoothing out with Theo, and he, Fergus, and Kerwin were finally finding a rhythm. That didn't make it easy. Theo was still just a baby and woke up several times every night. Fergus had insisted he be the one getting up every time, but Kerwin had refused. He wanted to contribute, and Theo was his son as much as he was Fergus's. It didn't matter that Fergus hadn't gone back to work yet. He was a full-time father most of the day while Kerwin got a break at training, and he deserved to have a good night's sleep as often as possible.

But that meant that Kerwin was exhausted most of the time, and it made it hard to focus. Thankfully, the trainers were aware of the situation, what with Jamison showing off pictures of his nephew almost as often as Kerwin. They were still in the beginning of their training, so they didn't do anything too dangerous, even when they trained in combat, which meant that Kerwin was safe even when he wasn't paying attention.

The physical lessons were fairly easy to get through, but the theoretical ones were harder. Kerwin could barely keep his eyes open, and he was pretty sure everyone knew it.

He peeked sideways at Wallace, who was staring ahead, but he didn't ask him what was going on again. If Wallace wanted to talk, he'd talk.

But Kerwin was worried about him. Wallace never liked to feel like a bother, and maybe that was why he hadn't said anything. Kerwin could imagine what was going on. After the scene Wallace's father had made the last time he'd been here, Kerwin was ready to bet pretty much everything he owned that the asshole was involved in Wallace's quietness. There was nothing Kerwin could do about the man, but he could be a listening ear if Wallace needed him to.

"Is your mate keeping you awake at night?" Cynthia teased once the lesson was over, and they filed out of the classroom.

"My son does," Kerwin answered.

She wrinkled her nose. "That's still really weird to hear."

"Why? A lot of people become parents at twenty-four."

"Yeah, but how many of them are council assassins?"

The team had met most of the assassins, and Payne and Greg lived with the group. That meant Kerwin knew a fair bit about them, including the fact that none had children. They'd kind of adopted Greg and Payne when they rescued them, but the two had already been in their late teens.

Kerwin swallowed. "Well, we're not assassins yet. I guess we'll see what happens once that changes."

"You'll take a step back?" Cynthia sounded stunned.

"Yeah. The most important thing in my life is my family. Don't get me wrong, I'd love to do this job and be useful, but if I have to choose, Theo and Fergus will always come first." Kerwin would never allow Theo to feel the way he had about his father's absence. He'd never let Fergus become bitter because he was never home. Kerwin could find many jobs, but he'd only ever have one mate and one chance to do things right with Theo. He wouldn't waste it.

"I don't understand, but I guess I don't have to," Cynthia said. She slapped Kerwin's shoulder. "Well, I'll see you tomorrow."

The way she said it caught Kerwin's attention. She'd put emphasis on the *tomorrow* part, but that was when they'd see each other next. Lessons were over for today, meaning Kerwin would go home soon.

He watched Cynthia as she reached a small group of other trainees. Both she, Seymour, and Hayden turned to look at him. They quickly turned back when they saw he was staring, but they didn't separate, instead whispering to each other.

They were hiding something.

Kerwin was curious and wanted to know what was happening. It was none of his business, though, so instead of going up to them and poking until they revealed what they were hiding, he looked around again. Wallace was digging into his backpack, hovering by the classroom door, probably waiting for Hawthorne. Kerwin needed to go home, but he also wanted to talk to Wallace and make sure everything was all right.

He quickly texted Fergus to warn him he'd be a bit late,

then leaned against the wall in the hallway and watched his friend.

Wallace's expression smoothed out, and his eyes lit up when Hawthorne came out of the room. Kerwin was too far away to hear what they were saying, but he could see the way they were with each other.

Wallace was shy and kept some distance between them, but Hawthorne couldn't look away from him, and he kept leaning closer. He never touched Wallace, and the few times he came close, he shook himself and moved back as if he caught himself before doing something he shouldn't do.

Kerwin didn't understand. Both Wallace and Hawthorne were adults, and Wallace was training to be a professional assassin. No one here would care if he dated a trainer, surely?

But Hawthorne clearly had limits and lines in the sand, and Kerwin respected that. He was curious if it was because of the trainer-trainee thing, and he might even ask Hawthorne about it eventually, but for now, his focus was on Wallace, who was smiling for the first time today.

Wallace chuckled, nodded, then stepped away from Hawthorne. He gave him a little wave before turning toward Kerwin. Kerwin kept his focus on Hawthorne, so he saw the trainer staring at Wallace's back for much longer than would be normal in this situation.

"You didn't have to wait for me," Wallace said when he reached Kerwin.

"I didn't have to, but I wanted to." Kerwin pushed away from the wall, and they moved down the hallway.

"I'm sure Fergus wants you home ASAP," Wallace pointed out.

"He does, but I texted him to warn him I'd be a bit late. Why don't you come home with me? Fergus will be happy to see you."

Usually, Kerwin had to push to get Wallace to visit. He

often used Theo as bait, and it always worked, but it was almost as if Wallace didn't want to be a bother.

This time, though, he grinned and nodded right away. "I'd love to."

Kerwin waited until they were in the car to bring up Wallace's father. "So, is your father the reason you've been so down lately?"

"When isn't he?" Wallace leaned against the window. "He's been calling me incessantly. He's pissed because I'm not answering, but I don't have to in order to know what he wants to tell me."

"Let me guess. He believes you should train harder."

"Mostly, he complains that I'm too weak and a disappointment. I read enough of that in his emails not to want to hear it from him personally."

"Then keep not answering."

"That was the plan. I know you want to talk about it, but I really don't."

Kerwin patted Wallace's knee. "No problem." They could be silent, and they were until they reached the building.

Kerwin parked in his spot, already smiling at the thought that his mate and their son were waiting for him inside. They'd have to find a new place soon, but for now, Fergus's apartment was big enough for the three of them.

"I wonder what's for dinner," he said as they rode the elevator up.

"Who's cooking?"

"Usually, Fergus does. You know I'm a disaster in the kitchen."

But Kerwin had been trying to learn. It wasn't easy, and he was angry at his mother for never allowing him in the kitchen when the cook was there, but he'd get over that, too. It was just one more thing in the pile of reasons he had to resent her.

"Yeah, it's better if he doesn't eat anything you cook,"

Wallace agreed. "But please tell me you've been taking care of the food at least every so often."

"I have. I promise I'm not letting him starve or work himself to death."

"Good."

The hallway was silent when they stepped out of the elevator. They walked to the door, and Kerwin frowned when he realized he could hear someone talking inside. Maybe Fergus had the TV on, but it wasn't quite the right sound.

Kerwin wasn't surprised to see he'd been right when he opened the door.

He frowned when he saw Cynthia sitting on his couch. She wasn't alone, and he looked around, seeing every single person they trained with, along with Jamison and even Kerwin's father.

"What's going on?" Kerwin asked, keeping his voice soft so he wouldn't wake up the baby if he was sleeping.

Fergus appeared from the kitchen. His cheeks were flushed as he made a beeline for Kerwin. "Surprise," he said. "Your friends wanted to have a party to celebrate Theo."

"And you," Hayden yelled from his spot on the couch.

Fergus's cheeks flushed. "And me. Anyway, they're here to celebrate."

Kerwin had been right. His friends *had* been hiding something.

Fergus hadn't known what to say when Wallace had called him to tell him that he and the other people who worked with Kerwin wanted to organize a small party to celebrate Kerwin finding his mate and becoming a father. Fergus hadn't been able to say no, especially when Wallace had promised he'd take care of everything. He'd promised Fergus wouldn't have to lift a finger and even that he'd clean the apartment once it was over. Fergus had been doing what he could to keep the apartment neat, but it was due for deep cleaning, so he'd been more than happy to say yes. It was also nice to see that even though Kerwin's mother was angry about their mating and the adoption, the other people in Kerwin's life were happy for him.

Even Kerwin's father had come. Fergus hadn't talked to him yet, but he would soon. He was the only supportive grandparent Theo would have other than Fergus's grandmother, and Fergus wanted the man to become part of their lives.

That didn't mean he wasn't nervous. He didn't know how to deal with parents and was afraid to make a mistake. They couldn't afford to lose Kerwin's father's support because Fergus wouldn't take another parent from Kerwin, which meant this meeting had to go well.

Fergus slipped into the bedroom, certain he'd heard Theo crying. It was a bit hard considering how many people were in his living room, but he was right. When he peeked into the crib, Theo's eyes were open, and he was grimacing, a sure sign he needed to be changed.

Fergus quickly did that. He'd become a pro at changing the baby, but for some reason, Kerwin was the only one who could calm Theo down when Fergus had already tried everything else. If Theo wasn't crying because he needed to be changed or fed, then there was almost no chance for Fergus to make him stop crying.

Theo relaxed once he was clean, but he wasn't going back to sleep just yet. Since the people in the living room were here to celebrate Theo as much as Kerwin's mating, Fergus decided to take Theo out. It would be good for him to be introduced to the people who were part of his father's life. Even though Fergus didn't know much about Kerwin's job, he knew enough to be able to tell that the people in his living room would be in their lives for a while. It wasn't exactly like a family, but it was the closest thing to a family Kerwin had.

So even though he wanted nothing more than to hide in his bedroom, he hiked Theo higher on his chest, sucked in a breath, and stepped out.

Only a few people noticed Theo, but every single one who did smiled. Kerwin was talking to his father in a corner of the crowded room, and Fergus decided it was time for Theo to meet his grandfather and for him to meet his father-in-law. It didn't matter how nervous he was. This needed to be done.

It wasn't that Fergus didn't want to meet Kerwin's father. He did, but he was afraid. Things didn't usually go well for him when it came to parents, and he didn't want to be hurt again. Kerwin had assured him that his father was happy for them, but how could Fergus be sure?

Kerwin looked up as Fergus reached him. He grinned when he saw Theo in Fergus's arm, and he looked so relaxed that Fergus found himself relaxing, too.

"Here they are," Kerwin told his father.

He put down his beer and grabbed Fergus, pulling him closer and wrapping an arm around his waist. Fergus balanced Theo against his chest with one hand while offering the other to Kerwin's father.

"It's a pleasure to meet you, sir."

Kerwin's father smiled. "It truly is a pleasure to meet you, Fergus. My son has told me so much about you that I feel I already know you."

Fergus wasn't sure what to say to that, so he limited himself to a smile. He'd never been great with people, and this situation wasn't any different except for the fact that even if he messed things up, Kerwin wasn't going anywhere.

They'd bonded. That meant that they'd be together for the rest of their lives, and he was happy about that.

He was also happy Kerwin couldn't run away and leave

him behind.

Kerwin wouldn't do that. Fergus knew it, but sometimes, it was nice to remind himself that they were bonded. He loved Fergus and Theo, and he'd never do anything to jeopardize their presence in his life.

"And please, call me Hurley," Kerwin's father continued. "Or Dad, like Kerwin does, but it's up to you. Just do what you're most comfortable with."

Fergus's mouth went dry. He'd never called anyone that, and he wasn't sure he could start at thirty-five. Still, it was nice to know he had the option, and he found himself smiling at Hurley more naturally. "I think I'll go with Hurley, at least for now."

Thankfully, Hurley didn't seem offended by Fergus's choice. "That's perfectly fine." He leaned closer. "And this is Theo," he said, looking at the baby.

Theo was staring around with wide eyes. He couldn't understand what was happening, but it didn't mean he wasn't interested in the many people he could see. Until now, his world had been restricted to Fergus, Kerwin, Wallace, and a handful of other people. This was a lot of new faces for him to deal with, so Fergus wouldn't be surprised if he started crying.

"It is," he told Hurley. "Hurley, meet your grandson."

Hurley's smile trembled. "There was a time in which I wasn't sure I'd ever have grandchildren," he whispered, gently touching the back of Theo's head. "And it would have been fine if Kerwin had decided he didn't want kids. I wouldn't have blamed him, and I certainly wouldn't have demanded he have kids even though he wasn't ready for it."

Kerwin groaned. "Can we not talk about her tonight?"

Hurley smiled at him. "Of course. I don't want to ruin this moment. Just know that I'm glad you found happiness."

Fergus stared at the two men. He'd never had this kind of

relationship with his father, and he never would because he didn't even know who the man was. He'd also never have this with his mother because there was no way he wanted to see her again after what she'd done to Theo and the way she'd behaved.

But Fergus wasn't completely alone. His grandmother had always been a steady presence in his life, and that hadn't changed. She didn't care that Fergus's mother — her daughter — didn't want to talk to him. She didn't care that Emily had given up her son. She wanted to be in Theo's life, to be a grandmother to him like she'd been to Fergus, and Fergus wanted both of them to have that.

That meant he and Kerwin would have to get her out of that house, which was something that made him anxious, but he'd deal with it. He wasn't giving up his grandmother, no matter who he had to fight to get her back.

"Kerwin told me what happened with your mother," Hurley said, his tone serious now.

Fergus grimaced. "It's not something I'm proud of."

"You don't have anything to be ashamed of. Your mother's behavior is entirely on her, not on you. Besides, considering how my wife treated Kerwin, maybe I should be ashamed, too."

"How about we agree not to be ashamed of the behavior of people we can't control?" Fergus offered. "The only behavior we can do something about is ours, and you're here. That's what's important, both for Theo and Kerwin."

Hurley nodded. "I can agree to that. But I'm sorry your family behaved the way they did and that you lost them. I want you to know that you're not alone. I already told Kerwin, but I want to tell you, too. I'm taking a step back from my work so I can focus on family."

Hurley was a healer, and from what Kerwin had explained, he'd been working a lot since Kerwin was a child. First it was to establish his practice, but now he worked with several other doctors and healers, so it should be fairly easy for him to find someone to cover his patients. "Theo will be glad to have you in his life, but you don't have to give up your job for that."

"I'm not giving up my job, and I'm not just doing this for Theo. I want to be a better grandfather than I was a father, but since we still have time, I also want to be a better father, both to Kerwin and you, if you'll take me."

Fergus couldn't help but smile. "I don't only take you, I welcome you."

His phone vibrated in his pocket, and he was a little bit relieved. This conversation had become heavy with feelings, and he had no idea how to deal with it.

"Will you take the baby? My phone is ringing," he said.

Hurley beamed and held out his arms. Fergus quickly transferred Theo into them, then took his phone out of his pocket. Even if Theo didn't want to stay where he was, Kerwin wasn't far. He'd take care of their son.

Fergus was surprised to see Kendra's name on his screen at this time of the evening. "I hope you have good news," he said as he stepped into a quieter corner.

The pregnant pause before Kendra answered told Fergus everything he needed to know. "Unfortunately, I don't," Kendra said. "I just got a call from your mother. She says your sister wants her son back."

Kerwin could tell something was wrong from Fergus's expression. He had no idea who was on the other side of the phone, but whatever they'd told Fergus, it wasn't good.

Kerwin and his father exchanged a glance. Kerwin's dad seemed happy to keep Theo, who was starting to fall asleep again, which hopefully meant Kerwin would be able to focus on his mate. Fergus was freaking out, even though he was trying his best to hide it from the people around them. Kerwin wanted to respect that, which meant that as soon as Fergus hung up, he'd drag him to their bedroom.

"That doesn't look good," Kerwin's father murmured.

"As soon as we think we're past one hurdle, another comes up."

Kerwin's father smiled at him. "That's what being adults usually means, unfortunately."

Kerwin glanced around. He doubted Fergus would be comfortable with so many people around him when he'd just gotten bad news, which meant something needed to be done.

Even though Kerwin wanted nothing more than to go straight to Fergus, he instead found Wallace and waved him closer. Wallace bounced toward him, a smile on his face that quickly vanished when he realized something was happening. Fergus had retreated to a corner of the room, but almost everyone here was a shifter with better hearing than humans and demons. They could probably tell something was up.

"What's going on?" Wallace asked.

"I'm not sure yet, but I think Fergus will need some space. Can you talk to everyone and ask them to leave?"

Wallace didn't hesitate. "Of course. A few of us will come back tomorrow to help clean up, so don't do anything tonight. They'll want to know everything is okay, though. What do I tell them?"

"I don't know yet."

"Well, remember that we're all here for you if you need any kind of help. Whatever it is, we're a team. We'll face it together."

Because they were becoming a family. There weren't many trainees, what with the program being secret and everything, and they spent every day together. Kerwin wasn't close to everyone, but it didn't matter. They were all there for the others.

It only took Wallace a few moments to go from group to group and explain that something had come up and the party needed to end. As soon as the others realized that whatever was happening was serious, they didn't linger. They didn't even come over to say goodbye and bother Kerwin or Fergus. They waved, made a few gestures that told Kerwin he needed to give them a call, and left. Wallace and Jamison were the last to go, and even though Jamison looked like he wanted to stay, he allowed Wallace to drag him away. Kerwin had no doubt he'd call eventually, but for now, being alone meant he could focus on Fergus.

"I can go if you want me to, but maybe it would be best for me to stay and take care of Theo," Kerwin's father said.

"Would you mind?"

"I wouldn't have offered if I did. Go to your mate, make sure he's all right. Theo and I will be in the kitchen, getting a bottle ready."

Once again, Kerwin was happy his father had proved himself to be so very different from his mother. She would have demanded to know what was going on and tried to get involved in whatever drama was happening, making it even more of an issue. Kerwin's father was a calm presence instead, and just having him there told Kerwin that whatever was happening, he and Fergus wouldn't have to face it alone.

Fergus was still in the corner, his face white as a sheet. Kerwin rushed to his side, giving in to his need to be with him now that he was sure Theo was safe.

He gently touched Fergus's back, and Fergus startled, twirling around to face him. His eyes were wide and damp looking, which made Kerwin want to grab whoever was hurting his mate and give them a good shake.

"What is it?" he asked.

"Kendra? Kerwin just got here, so I'm going to put you on

speaker," Fergus said.

Kerwin didn't hear what Kendra answered, but he didn't have to. As Fergus put her on speaker, he gave Kerwin a curt explanation. "Kendra got a phone call from my mother. Apparently, Emily wants Theo back."

The bottom of Kerwin's stomach dropped. "What? Why would she want Theo back? She was adamant that she didn't want a demon child."

"Kerwin," Kendra said on the other side of the phone.

"I'm sorry, but I don't understand," Kerwin told her. "She signed away her parental rights. Is there anything she can do to get Theo back? Where are we with the adoption process?" Kerwin couldn't allow this to happen. He wouldn't lose any part of his family beyond his mother, but especially not Theo. Theo was his son, and he'd fight to keep him.

"She doesn't have a leg to stand on," Kendra said.

Kerwin relaxed, but only a fraction. This was still too much of a mess for him to be comfortable. "What does she think she's doing, then?"

"I didn't talk to Emily but to her mother. I have the suspicion that she's the one behind this rather than her daughter."

"I have to agree," Fergus intervened. "This is something my mother would do. I wouldn't be surprised if she learned that Kerwin's family is wealthy and thinks she can get money from them through Theo."

Kerwin hadn't even thought of that. His family was wealthy, but *he* wasn't. Just like the other trainees, he got paid by the council, but not much. Once they became assassins, they'd be paid better, but for now, Kerwin couldn't afford to pay off Fergus's mother, even though he and Fergus were comfortable enough not to worry about paying the bills.

Beyond that, Kerwin didn't *want* to pay her off. She was the kind of person who'd come back for more again and again, and that wasn't something Kerwin wanted to deal with.

"What do we do, then?" Fergus asked.

Kendra sounded sure of herself as she answered. "You let me deal with it. I'm pretty sure she's bluffing, and I want to call her out on that bluff. I'll tell her that we don't have a problem facing her in front of a judge. She'll have to get a lawyer, although I'm not sure she'll be able to find anyone, considering the case. Of course, she could lie to them and not give them every detail, so we'll have to see. I don't want the two of you to worry, though. I had to tell you what's happening, but Theo isn't going anywhere. He's your son, even though the adoption papers haven't been processed yet."

"You're sure?" Kerwin asked. He needed to hear the words.

"I am."

"I could try talking to Emily," Fergus offered.

"I don't think it would change anything if your mother is behind this, but feel free to try. Let me know how it goes, all right? In the meantime, don't worry too much. I have everything in hand."

Kerwin wanted to drag Fergus into his arms and hold on to him, but as soon as Fergus hung up with Kendra, he dialed another number. Kerwin wasn't surprised and moved closer, wrapping an arm around Fergus's shoulders. Fergus leaned against him, his phone close enough to Kerwin that Kerwin could hear the other side of the conversation.

"Fergus?" Emily asked when she answered. She sounded surprised.

"What are you doing?" Fergus snapped.

"What? I don't know what you're talking about."

"My lawyer got a phone call. Mom said that you want Theo back."

There was a moment of silence, and Kerwin held his breath. Would Emily agree that she wanted her son back? Why would she do that when she hadn't wanted him in the first place? It wasn't like he was different now. He was still half demon, and he always would be.

"I didn't say anything to your lawyer," Emily protested. "I'm on vacation."

"Then why did Mom call her?"

"She tried to make me change my mind before I left," Emily explained. "She started telling me that maybe we gave up the baby too soon and that we should try getting him back, but I don't want him."

Kerwin didn't like the way she talked about Theo, but he was relieved she hadn't changed her mind.

"If you don't want him, what's this all about? Why is Mom doing this?" Fergus asked.

Unfortunately, Kerwin doubted anyone could explain that woman's behavior. He didn't care to try, either. He just wanted to keep his family safe and for the people who clearly didn't love them to leave them alone. Was that too much to ask?

"I don't know, Fergus," Emily answered with a whine. "I never know why she does the things she does."

Fergus licked his lips. This had been a good day and an even better evening, but like always, his mother had ruined everything. All the warmth and strength he'd gotten from knowing he wasn't alone anymore had leaked out of his body, and now, he dreaded the rest of the evening.

He wanted to find his mother and scream at her. He wanted to rage that she was ruining everything. He couldn't afford to do that, though, which meant he needed to focus on something else. "I won't try to keep you away from Theo if you want to see him," he said slowly. He'd thought about this before, and he and Kerwin had talked, so Fergus didn't feel guilty about offering this.

"Theo?" Emily sounded distracted, which wasn't a surprise considering she was on vacation. She'd put Theo out of her mind as soon as she left the hospital, and she probably hadn't thought of him twice since then.

"The child you gave birth to. The child I adopted. If you want a relationship with him, I won't keep him away from you. You're his mother, at least biologically. If you truly changed your mind and want some kind of relationship with him, I'll be okay with that, with conditions."

"I don't want anything from that kid," Emily said. "I left him, didn't I? As far as I'm concerned, he's not my son. He's yours, and I'll be a horrible aunt, never mind a mother."

Fergus couldn't say he disagreed. "So you truly had nothing to do with this?"

"I told you I didn't," Emily said with a huff.

Fergus could hear people talking and laughing around her, and he wondered where she was. He hadn't even thought to ask, and to be honest, he didn't care.

"I have to go," Emily continued. "If you want an explanation, you should ask Mom. I'm sure she can tell you what she was thinking because I have no idea, and I don't care."

Emily hung up before Fergus could add anything. He stared at his phone, trying to make sense of what had happened.

Kendra had said that his mother had been the one to contact her on behalf of Emily. She'd explained Emily wanted Theo back and that she was ready to fight for him, but Kendra hadn't believed it.

Fergus didn't, either.

If Emily had changed her mind, he would have given her a chance, but she'd never cared about anyone but herself. Having a child hadn't changed that, so it hadn't been a surprise to find out she was out of town and having fun. She didn't want to be a mother, and she wasn't. She clearly didn't want anything to do with Theo, which meant she hadn't been the one behind that phone call.

Fergus's mother had been.

What was she doing? What was she trying to get from all of this? Maybe he'd been right that his mother was doing this because she wanted money. That was all she ever cared about, and he doubted she'd suddenly grown a heart and changed her mind about demons being filthy creatures.

Fergus called his mother next. There was no one he wanted to hear from less, but he needed to get this over with. The sooner he did, the sooner he, Kerwin, and Theo could go back to their normal lives.

"What do you want?" his mother snapped when she answered.

"I should be the one asking you that. Why did you call my lawyer?"

"She called you, then? She said she didn't have to because nothing I can say will change the fact that you're the baby's father. I knew she was lying."

"She wasn't. You're not getting Theo, no matter who you call. I need you to leave my family and me alone."

"*I* am your family. I'm your mother, and you'll do what I say."

Normally, Fergus would. He was ashamed to think of how he'd behaved before, but he wanted to keep the peace.

Not anymore. He didn't care if his mother yelled at him. He didn't care if she got angry and threatened him. Before, he'd had everything to lose if he'd gone against her. He hadn't wanted to lose his family, even though it was a shitty one.

But his current family was good. More than that, Theo didn't deserve to be used the way Fergus's mother was planning. The more Fergus thought about it, the more he was convinced that she was doing this for the money. He wasn't about to give her what she wanted, but he was terrified of what would happen if she actually took this to a judge. Kendra was convinced it wouldn't work, but what if it did? What if Fergus's mother got Theo?

Fergus had grown up with her, so he knew how she'd treat Theo. Actually, it would probably be worse for Theo since he was half demon, and Fergus's mother hated demons. There was no way she'd changed her mind about that, especially not so quickly.

"I'm done with you," he said with a growl. "I don't want to see you ever again. I don't want to hear from you ever again. You'd better leave my family alone because if you don't, I'll destroy you."

She snorted. "You and what army?"

"I don't need an army. I know you want something from me, but I won't give it to you. I'll make sure that whatever judge ends up with this knows how you raised me and what you and Emily did to me. I'll make sure they know that Emily doesn't want to be a mother and that she was okay with me becoming Theo's father. No one will give you this baby."

"I could make things easier for you. Stop all of this before it happens."

And there it was. "You want money?"

"Your demon is loaded. I looked into him."

It was fairly easy these days with social media, and Fergus's mother spent hours on her phone scrolling and spying on people. "I wouldn't care even if he was a millionaire. You're not getting anything from either of us. Leave us alone. I'll see you in front of a judge if you don't."

Fergus hung up. It wasn't as satisfying to press a spot on his screen as to slam down the receiver like he would have with a landline, but it didn't matter. He was already dialing yet another number.

Through it all, Kerwin had stood next to him, taking his weight and listening to everything Fergus was saying. He'd had questions for Kendra, but now, he was silent, lending Fergus his strength because he knew he needed it.

Thankfully, this was the last phone call Fergus had to make. Once it was out of the way, he'd be done with his mother. He hadn't been lying when he'd said he never wanted to see her again, and he hoped he wouldn't have to. He'd certainly make sure Theo would never have to meet her. The baby didn't deserve that much nastiness and hate.

"Oh, Fergus," Fergus's grandmother said when she answered. "I'm really sorry."

"You know what's happening?"

"I didn't before, but I heard your mother on the phone with you. What is she doing this time?"

Now that Fergus had Theo, he could imagine how bad his grandmother felt about his mother's behavior. She had to wonder where she'd gone wrong and what she'd done to raise her daughter like this. Fergus didn't think it was something his grandmother had done. Sometimes, people were bad, and there was nothing anyone could do. His mother was an adult, and she was making her own decisions. *She'd* decided to do this to Fergus, and Fergus's grandmother had nothing to do with it.

"She wants money. She's threatening to take Theo away if we don't pay her."

"I'm not surprised. And just wait until she finds out I changed my will."

Fergus spluttered. "You did?"

"Considering how she and Emily have been behaving, I don't want them to get anything. I have no doubt they'll fight it when I die, but I don't care. Almost everything will go to you and Theo."

Maybe Fergus's mother knew about it and thought his grandmother would change her mind if she had the baby. She might even try to use Theo to force her mother to change her will back. By this point, nothing Fergus's mother could do would surprise him.

"You shouldn't have to stay with them. Why don't you move in with Kerwin and me?"

"Are you sure? You're newly bonded, and I wouldn't want to impose."

"I'm sure." Fergus and Kerwin had talked about it, and they both agreed. Fergus's grandmother was old and didn't have many years left. Fergus wanted them to be happy and for Theo to grow up with his grandmother close by. Besides, with the three of them, they'd be able to find a bigger home.

"Consider me packed, then," Fergus's grandmother said. "We can start looking for a home because I'm not moving into your apartment. Where would I sleep? On the couch?"

Fergus grinned. At least one good thing would come out of this.

CHAPTER SEVEN

"I'll pick her up," Kerwin told Fergus.

He leaned over him on the bed and kissed his forehead, then Theo's.

Fergus was sitting with his back against the headboard, Theo curled on his chest. It was the only place where Theo would sleep without crying. Every time Fergus tried to put him down in his crib, Theo started screaming.

Both Fergus and Kerwin were exhausted. Theo's doctor had said it was a bit of colic, but it sounded as if Theo was dying every time it started. Fergus had even asked Kerwin's father, who'd confirmed what the doctor had said. There was only one thing they could do.

Wait for it to pass.

Kerwin was lucky. Every day, he left the house and had some respite. The same couldn't be said for Fergus, which probably was why he'd wanted to come along to pick up his grandmother. Kerwin was glad he wouldn't be coming. He didn't want Fergus to have to deal with his mother, even though the mess of her trying to get Theo was already over.

Kendra was right. Fergus's mother had stopped trying before they could truly start to worry about what would happen. Kerwin didn't know if it was because she couldn't afford a lawyer, but whatever the case, he didn't care. Kendra had put a push on the adoption papers going through, which meant that hopefully, in no more than a few weeks, Theo would officially be their son, and the poor baby wouldn't have to deal with his grandmother ever again.

But all of this meant that Fergus's mother was pissed, and she was taking it out on her own mother. She wasn't violent, but Fergus's grandmother had repeated some of the things her daughter had said, and it was horrifying.

The three of them had put their heads together and had found a house that would work for their family. It had a small mother-in-law cottage outside of the main house, and Fergus's grandmother had been delighted. When Fergus suggested she move into the main house with them so she'd be closer, she'd snorted and said something about them being newly mated that had made Fergus blush.

Kerwin couldn't wait to meet her.

"Call me as soon as you're with her," Fergus ordered.

"I promise I will. Don't worry about anything. Your grandmother will be fine." And Kerwin would have a few choice words for Fergus's mother. Fergus didn't need to know about that, though.

Kerwin kissed Fergus's forehead again. "Try to get some rest. I'll take over as soon as I'm back."

It wouldn't be long. Fergus's grandmother had bought the house they'd found, putting both Fergus and Kerwin's names on the deed. She'd live in the cottage until she died but wanted the house to be theirs. That was when Kerwin had realized that she was wealthy, too, and it made him wonder why Fergus's mother needed money. Had she treated her own mother so badly that Fergus's grandmother didn't want to give her even a penny? Kerwin wouldn't be surprised if that was the case.

Fergus's grandmother was moving into the cottage today, but it would take a few more days for Fergus and Kerwin to move out of the apartment. Kerwin's team had already agreed to help, so it wouldn't take them long, and Kerwin couldn't wait. This felt like another step forward in their life together, and while everything was still a mess, the most important thing wasn't.

They were a family. They loved each other.

He left the apartment and drove as quickly as he could to Fergus's grandmother. She'd already told Kerwin to call her Grandma, and he had every intention of doing just that. He didn't have grandparents anymore, but he had fond memories of them, and he felt he was getting them back.

When he parked in front of the address Fergus had given him, it was to hear a woman screaming inside. He grinned, knowing that Fergus's grandmother must have told her daughter she was moving out. They'd been sneaky about it until now, but the secret was out.

"I'm not letting you leave," a woman screamed.

Kerwin couldn't hear the answer, but he didn't have to. He climbed out of his car and rushed toward the front door, not wanting Fergus's grandmother to have to listen to one more second of this.

He knocked, then waited. When the door opened, it revealed the woman he'd crossed paths with at the hospital. He'd been sure she was Fergus's mother, and he was right.

It took her a moment to recognize him. When she did, her eyes widened and her nostrils flared. "What the fuck are you doing here?" she demanded to know.

Kerwin smiled. He wasn't doing it on purpose to scare her, but seeing the fear in her gaze was a nice secondary effect. He was just happy, and nothing she could do or say would change that. "I'm here to pick up Fergus's grandmother."

"You're not taking my mother," Fergus's mother said, pointing her finger at Kerwin. "I'm not letting you."

"You're not letting him do anything," another woman said from behind Fergus's mother. She pushed Fergus's mother to the side, then thrust a bag into Kerwin's arms. "I only have a few bags. You can start by taking this one to the car."

Kerwin already liked Fergus's grandmother. He winked at

her, then went to put the bag into the car. The two women were still bickering at the door when he came back.

"I'm your *mother*," Fergus's grandmother was saying. "You don't get to make decisions for me, especially because you always make the worst decisions."

"I've only ever wanted the best for you," Fergus's mother protested.

"You only ever want what's best for *you*. I don't know what I did wrong with you, and at this point, I don't care. I want you out of my life and my grandson's and great-grandson's lives. We're all done with you." She was holding another bag, and she stomped away from the house and toward the car.

Kerwin watched her go. She was tiny, with short gray hair and eyes that blazed with anger. He wouldn't want to cross her, and he was glad her anger wasn't directed at him.

"You're wrong if you think I'll allow you to do this," Fergus's mother hissed.

"I believe your mother was clear. She wants out of this place, and I don't blame her, even though I only met you twice. You're a bitch, lady." Kerwin normally wouldn't call anyone a bitch, but it had never fit so well.

"How *dare* you?"

Kerwin looked back to see that Fergus's grandmother was climbing into the car. He'd noticed another three bags by the front door, and he was relieved these seemed to be the only things she was taking with her. They could come back later if she'd missed something, although Kerwin really hoped they wouldn't have to.

He grabbed the bags and leaned closer to Fergus's mother. She sucked in a breath and took a step back as if she expected him to attack her, and she wasn't that far from the truth. He'd never hated anyone the way he hated her.

"You're going to leave my family and me alone," he said slowly to be sure she understood. "You'll never try to get

Theo again, and you'll never contact Fergus. The same goes for your daughter. The two of you need to leave us alone."

"I'm not scared of you."

"You should be. You see, I'm training to be a professional assassin. Do you really think I'd hesitate to kill you if you push me?"

Normally, Kerwin wouldn't have revealed that to anyone, especially not Fergus's mother. No one would believe her if she tried to tell them his secret, though, and he wanted her to be afraid of him. He hoped it would be enough to keep her away.

"You wouldn't do it," she said, her voice shaking.

"Are you sure you want to find out?"

Kerwin was done with this. He turned, never looking back as he strode toward the car where Fergus's grandmother was waiting for him. Hopefully, Fergus's mother had gotten the hint that she needed to stay away. Kerwin wouldn't hesitate to come back to have another conversation with her if that wasn't the case, even though he didn't want to. Now that this was over, he wanted to focus on the most important thing in his life.

His family.

ABOUT THE AUTHOR

Catherine is the creator of several series, most of them paranormal, including the Whitedell Pride Series and the Gillham Pack Series. While she graduated in translation, she decided to go the writer's way because it was more fun to create her own stories and characters.

She's been living in Italy for more than twenty years, but she's a daughter of the North—Belgium to be precise—and she misses it so much that she's already planning to move back.

She loves pizza—probably too much—her son, her pets, and of course, books. She sneaks some reading time into her schedule every time she has five minutes free from writing, demands from her various pets and son, and lastly, housework.

Connect with her:

lievens.catherine@gmail.com
BookBub: https://www.bookbub.com/authors/catherine-lievens
Website: https://authorcatherinelievens.com/
Facebook: https://www.facebook.com/catherine.lievens.9
Facebook Group: https://www.facebook.com/groups/411788002341528/
Twitter: https://twitter.com/authorCLievens
Newsletter: http://eepurl.com/c-uvKn

www.ingramcontent.com/pod-product-compliance
Lightning Source LLC
Chambersburg PA
CBHW060630130626
46555CB00002B/734